Frozen with fear, Jesse couldn't seem to take his eyes off the square-cut barrel.

There was no time to wonder what he'd ever done to inspire Rasheed to point a gun at his chest. He'd heard stories about gang members who hunted down boys who'd thought better of joining, but surely. . .

"Say your prayers, fool," Rasheed growled.

Something told him he was going to need prayers. Lots of them. But even before Jesse had a chance to search his mind for one, instinct forced him to raise his hands in a gesture of helpless supplication, and turn his head to protect his eyes from the flare of bright white light that flashed from the muzzle.

He'd heard the sound hundreds, thousands of times, maybe, on TV, in the movie theater. None of it had prepared him for the ear-blasting, rib-wracking explosion that cracked the quiet night. Nothing could have prepared him for the pain, either.

ALEESHA CARTER writes in the living room of a rustic Pennsylvania mountain cabin. She credits the sights and sounds on the other side of her picture window—woodlands, waterfalls, and wildlife—with her "God is present, and all is good" mind-set.

Soft Beats
My Heart

Aleesha Carter

Heartsong Presents

This book is dedicated to Rebecca Germany and Steve Reginald, whose faith in the salability of my work helped make an author of me, and to Mike Sackett, whose critiques helped make that work salable.

A note from the Author:
I love to hear from my readers! You may write to me at the following address: Aleesha Carter
Author Relations
P.O. Box 719
Uhrichsville, OH 44683

ISBN 1-57748-010-4

SOFT BEATS MY HEART

Cover illustration by Brian Bowman.

PRINTED IN THE U.S.A.

prologue

Sadie Burke chewed the tip of her fine-tipped sable brush and squinted at the streaks of white highlight she'd just painted on a Granny Smith apple. *It's good*, she thought, tilting her head to study the work, *but it needs something. . .*

A sunbeam spilled over the window sill and formed a shimmering golden puddle at her feet, giving the aged hardwood floor the look of caramelized sugar. *That's what this painting needs. . .the warm hue of wood. . .*

"That bowl of fruit looks real enough to eat; if I were you, I'd quit painting still lifes and landscapes and draw myself a husband," her sister said, dropping her purse on the empty chair near the door.

One hand over her hammering heart, Sadie closed her eyes and inhaled deeply. "I declare, Hannah, Mama must have named you after a hurricane, the way you blow into a room. You scared me half to death!"

Hannah was far too busy inspecting her younger sister's latest work of art to pay any mind to the half-hearted chastisement. One fist on her hip and the other nestled beneath her chin, she nodded. "This one's good, Sadie, real good." Then, a portrait, leaning against the far wall caught her eye. "Say, he's *cute*. Is he real, or a figment of your artist's imagination?"

Sadie put the paintbrush in the tray at the bottom of her easel. "He's real all right, and you know him every bit as well as I do. That's none other than Floyd Barnes. He's got his own office now, you know, and his mama wants a portrait of her boy in the waiting room, so his clients will be—"

"*This* is ornery li'l Floyd Barnes?" Hannah interrupted. "The same Floyd Barnes who used to make paper airplanes out of Sunday school workbook pages to throw at the back of my head?" Her grin broadened and she wiggled her eyebrows. "I am *impressed*."

Sadie laughed softly. "What impresses you most, big sister? His Harvard law degree? His fancy office in the World Trade Center? His elegant condo overlooking the Inner Harbor?"

Hannah's big eyes narrowed with suspicion. "Floyd Barnes has all of *that*? Go *on*!"

Sadie nodded. "It's true. Every word." She winked. "He drives a red Porsche, too."

A grin lifted one corner of Hannah's mouth. "Is he married?"

"Nope. . .but you shouldn't be asking. You may have no idea where Calvin ran off to, but you're still a married woman."

The playful smile vanished from Hannah's face. "Painting isn't your only talent, little sister. You're a master at souring a sweet mood." She joined her purse in the chair near the door. "I haven't heard from that no-good husband of mine for nearly three years." She held up her hand and formed the Girl Scout salute. "Next year, I'm gonna use my tax refund to hire a lawyer and—"

"'What the Good Lord hath joined together, let no man put asunder. . .'"

"Easy for you to say," Hannah chided, frowning. "Doesn't the Bible also make allowance for the person who was left, the person who was innocent, the person who did everything she could to make her marriage work, only to have that two-timing, selfish man. . ." Her voice broke.

Sadie felt shame burn her cheeks. *Sometimes*, she scolded herself, *your self-righteousness is downright nauseating!* Being stood up by her prom date and then being left at the altar hardly compared to being left with two growing kids to feed and clothe, a mortgage to pay, car payments. . .

Unable to meet Hannah's wounded gaze, she retrieved her paintbrush. *What is it about Burke women*, Sadie asked herself, *that makes 'em end up manless*? Her grandfather had died while Granny still carried their fourth child in her womb, and her own father had deserted his family while Sadie still wore diapers. Her mother had eventually married again, only to lose her husband to a heart attack. Sighing, Sadie dipped the point of the brush into the white paint.

"You going to the church social this Saturday?" she asked, hoping to change the subject of missing husbands.

"Course I am!" Hannah replied, brightening. "I promised Pastor Harrison I'd bring my world-famous potato salad."

Sadie smiled, marveling at her sister's ability to bounce back from moods that would overpower most women. But her sister's grin never quite reached her eyes. Draw yourself a husband, Hannah had said when she'd come into the room. *That's the* only *way I'll ever get that near a man again. . . !*

Silently, she recited the pledge she'd made on the long, lonely night when she would have become Mrs. Evan Maxwell: "The only good man to ever walk this earth died on a cross; if you want happiness in this life, live for *Him*. . ."

one

"Jesse Turner, I flat out don't know what I'm going to do with you."

The boy slouched lower in his chair and stared at some unknown spot on the worn carpet beneath his Nike Aires.

"What's your daddy gonna say when he finds out what you've gone and done *this* time?" The clock on the wall ticked once, twice, three times before the giant in the three-piece suit slammed a fist onto his blotter, rattling the pens and pencils in his *Baltimore Orioles* mug and the nameplate that read *Arthur James Johnson, Principal*. "I asked you a question, Mr. Turner!"

The boy met the man's eyes. "I dunno what my daddy's gonna say."

Mr. Johnson rose to his full six-foot four-inch height, planted both meaty palms on the desktop, and leaned his considerable bulk into the space that separated him from Jesse. "Sit up straight and look at me when I talk to you," he growled.

The young man shifted uneasily in his seat, tugging at the cuffs of his baggy T-shirt. "Yessir, Mistah Johnson," the boy muttered.

"What's that?"

"I said, Yes sir, Mister Johnson."

Suddenly, Principal Johnson straightened and faced the window behind his desk. "I've had an eye on you since September," he said, his voice softer. "You're a bright kid, Jesse. Help me understand. . ." The big man turned slowly, a frown furrowing his fuzzy blond brows. "Tell me, son, what's wrong?"

In response, the teenager scrubbed his face with both

hands, shrugged, and breathed a long hollow sigh.

The weathered leather chair creaked in protest as Johnson seated himself once more. With calm deliberation, he folded both huge hands atop a file marked *Turner, Jesse S.* "Now, I realize it was tough, losing your mama the way you did. . ."

Jesse lowered his head, focused on that unknown spot again.

"But it's been *three years*, son," the principal continued in a gentler tone. He patted the folder. "Says here you've been nothing but trouble since sixth grade. . .sassing your teachers, bullying your classmates, skipping school. . ." He tapped the handle of the tiny pocketknife Coach Donaldson had taken from Jesse in the locker room, sending it spinning in a slow, lazy circle. "It's getting worse every year. And this isn't the first time you've threatened someone."

"But he tried to steal my radio!" Jesse protested, bolting upright in his chair. "He just reached in my locker an'—"

Johnson thrust a thick forefinger at the boy. "First of all, you don't know for certain Sam was going to *steal* anything. And second," he said, "you aren't even supposed to *have* a radio in your locker." His pale blue eyes narrowing, he added, "There are plenty of things you're not supposed to have on campus. . ." He ignored Jesse's sigh. "You know the rules, Turner, and one of those rules is 'No weapons.'"

"It's only a li'l bitty Boy Scout knife," Jesse muttered.

"The size or type of weapon is of no concern to me, Mr. Turner. I repeat: You know the rules." He closed his eyes and ran a hand through his thinning blond waves, then arched a brow. He picked up the pocketknife. "I have grounds to expel you, you know."

For an instant, fear glittered in Jesse's dark eyes. But he blinked it back, exhaled another bored sigh, and tucked in one corner of his mouth.

"I've talked 'til I'm hoarse, but your attitude makes it clear you have no intention of getting with the program." Johnson leaned forward slightly, his voice a near whisper when he said, "You've been a problem since your sweet mama was buried."

"Yo mama!" Jesse muttered, sarcastically.

"Now you listen to me, young man. You may think it's funny to speak in that tone about your mother, but I think it's revolting and disgusting. I *knew* your mother, son, and she was a living saint!"

Jesse slumped lower in his chair as Johnson's eyes narrowed. "Here's a piece of advice you'd be wise to take, Mr. Turner: You will *not* speak disrespectfully about your mother in *my* presence, because *I* will not tolerate it. She was a wonderful woman, and she deserves better. Is that clear?"

Johnson shook his head, leaned back in his chair. "I've known your daddy since we played football at Maryland, Jesse. I knew Coral, too. And I know how much losin' her hurt you. . .*and* your dad." He paused, then frowned. "Can't you see it's tearin' him up, watchin' what's becoming of you, day by day? Can't you see he's as lost and confused as you are, because he believes he didn't just lose his wife. . .he thinks he's losin' you, too."

Johnson paused, hoping his words would cause some reaction in the angry young man. When he saw none, he said through clenched teeth, "Let me tell you a thing or two, Mr. Turner. Up 'til now, you've been your daddy's problem. But you're a freshman here at Bradley Senior High now, and as such, you're my problem. But you won't let me help you. . ."

The icy tone in the man's otherwise jovial voice caught the boy's full attention. For the first time since being summoned to the office, Jesse Turner met Art Johnson's eyes.

"I've looked the other way," the man continued, "let you get away with a few things this year because, quite frankly, I was hoping and praying you'd get your act together." He closed the folder, as if closing a long-distressing subject. "Way I see it, there's just one ray of hope left. . ."

❧

Sadie Burke leafed through the file for the third time since it had been delivered earlier in the week. The youngsters recommended to attend the Betina Thornton School had problems, true, but few had a history less promising than Jesse Turner's. But why should she get so emotionally involved? Turner would just be one more bubble in the already boiling cauldron of troubled girls and boys.

She glanced at her Timex. In ten minutes, she'd be face to face with the unruly youth. . .and his widowed father. Sighing, she turned her attention back to the file, and reread the entry that said Jesse's mother had died of breast cancer three years ago. Since then, she discovered, frowning as she leafed through the pages, he'd been written up for vandalism, truancy, verbal and physical attacks on classmates. This last incident—threatening an upper classman—had almost gotten the boy expelled from school. At the recommendation of principal Johnson, Jesse Turner was being considered a candidate for enrollment at Thornton.

The mental picture of the hulking ex-Baltimore Colt hovered in her mind. Drafted by the team straight out of college, a knee injury had put an early end to Johnson's stellar sports career after only four seasons. Having majored in education at the University of Maryland, the quarterback changed occupations. . .and went into teaching. Hard work and dedication earned him the recognition of peers and superiors alike; within five years, he'd become principal of Sadie's former high school, where he quickly won the hearts of teachers on his staff. . .and his students. She couldn't think of a single person who didn't admire and respect the aging football star. If somebody as tough and capable as Art Johnson had given up on the boy and sought out her help instead. . .

A gentle knock at the door interrupted her thoughts. Sadie's secretary poked her head into the office. "Your ten o'clock is here," Shirley Howard whispered. "You want me to ask them to wait?"

Closing the file folder, Sadie smiled tentatively and walked quickly to the opaque-windowed door. Opening it wide, she winked at her secretary and friend. "No thanks, Shirl, I'll see them now." Still smiling, her attention divided by the man and the boy who sat side by side on the imitation leather sofa in the waiting room, Sadie stepped aside and waved them inside. "Sadie Burke," she said, extending her hand in welcome to the father.

"Solon Turner," he responded, raising and lowering her arm like a pump handle. With a nod, he indicated the boy. "And this is my son, Jesse."

She grasped the boy's hand, though he hadn't offered it. "It's nice to meet you. Please, won't you both have a seat?"

Mechanically, father and son sat in the upholstered chairs in front of her desk as she took quick inventory: Jesse wore clean, hip-rider jeans and a soft flannel shirt over his black T-shirt. She'd inhaled the crisp scent of laundry detergent and fabric softener moments ago as he'd swaggered past her. His father, in a gray suit and starched bright-white shirt, stood head and shoulders taller than his son. Sadie wondered who cared for these men so well, since Mrs. Turner had died years earlier.

"May I get either of you a soda?"

"I'll have a Pepsi," Jesse said, slouching in the chair.

She saw a muscle in Mr. Turner's jaw tighten as he glared at his son. Quirking an eyebrow, Sadie stepped up to the clothes tree in the corner, slipped off her amber suit jacket, and hung it on a brass peg. Rolling up the cuffs on her white oxford blouse, she plopped unceremoniously into her own chair.

"We buy store-brand sodas to save money," she explained, taking a two-liter bottle from the tiny fridge beside her desk to fill two paper cups. "Sorry," she said, handing them each a drink, "no ice."

As Jesse reached for his cup, his father's large, dark hand encircled his wrist. "What do you say to the nice lady?" he asked through clenched teeth.

Rolling his eyes, the boy blew a stream of air through his

lips. "Thank you. Thank you very much," he singsonged. "You are a very kind lady."

Shaking his head, Turner released his son.

Sadie leaned her elbows on Jesse's file. "It isn't easy, is it?" she asked him.

He moved nothing but his eyes, but she read the what-are-you-babbling-about? expression on his smug young face.

"I'm talking about your bad-boy rep. Is it as much work as it appears to be?"

The directness of her tone and attitude commanded attention, so much so that even Jesse couldn't ignore her. He cut her a quick glance and shrugged one shoulder. "Whatever. . ."

She tapped his file with a manicured fingernail, then aimed the same finger at him. "I know all about you, Jesse Turner, so let's get one thing straight right up front: I pay respect to *my* elders, and I expect to get it from those younger than I. From this point forward, when I address you, you will call me Miss Burke." She paused, folded her hands on the desktop. "You got that?"

Raising both brows, Jesse tucked in one corner of his mouth, as if to say, *Who do you think you are?* Instead, he said, "Yes, Miss Burke."

"If you prefer," she continued in a lighter tone, "you can call me. . .ma'am." She punctuated the suggestion with a grin and a wink.

Sadie ignored Jesse's father, who hid a smirk behind a big, work-hardened hand. *Yes, Mr. Turner, I'm getting the better of him. . .for the moment.* She'd been a social worker long enough to recognize a tough nut when she saw one. *But don't get your hopes up too high,* she silently warned the father. *We've got a long row to hoe before we make any headway with this one. . .*

"Why did you bring a knife to school, Jesse? I'm sure you knew it was against the rules."

He shrugged the other shoulder.

Crinkling her brow and pursing her lips, she said, "Are

you always this rude and inconsiderate, or are you just having a bad day?"

The baleful expression Jesse sent her clearly said he expected to be treated like an adult, even if had no intention of acting like one. But she'd seen the look before. Too many times. "You might *think* you're all grown up at fourteen, young man, but right now, you're acting like a spoiled little brat."

Again he rolled his eyes.

She walked around to the front of her desk, perched on its corner, and leaned in close. "You want me to treat you like an equal, Jesse?"

He met her eyes with a daring defiance. "I just want out of this place." That said, he focused on the door.

Oh, but he's an angry young'un, she mentally quoted her Granny, wondering as she did what series of events had put such fury into eyes that should, at this point in a young man's life, gleam with anticipation of the future.

Gently, Sadie squeezed his shoulder. "I happen to know you survived the Art Johnson Guided Tour of Juvie Hall. I also happen to know you've seen all there is of Thornton." With the tip of her forefinger, she gently lifted his chin and forced him to meet her eyes. "You want to be treated like an adult, Jesse? Well, then, act like one! Make a grown-up decision. It's your future at stake, after all." She dropped her hand back into her lap as she let the importance of her words sink in.

An instant of vulnerability flickered across his face, gentling the hard-earned tough-guy expression. *Mr. Johnson was right to give him a look at Juvie Hall*, she admitted as she watched the boy struggle with the memory of seeing the frightened faces of too many kids crowded into the dark, dank old building that served as juvenile hall down on Holliday Street. Johnson knew what he was doing, all right, forcing kids like Jesse to see life as it could be if they didn't walk a different walk.

Jesse's pout made Sadie see him as he might have looked

three years ago, before his mother's death turned his happy little-boy world upside down.

"Thornton's better than Juvie, I guess," he said dully.

She smiled. "By the end of the week, you'll *know* it's better." Standing, Sadie crossed to the door and opened it. "Now, would you mind waiting outside while your father and I discuss the financial arrangements?"

Immediately, Jesse got to his feet, paper cup in his hand, and walked toward the reception area. He hesitated for a moment in the doorway. "Mind if I get a refill first?" he asked, grinning slightly.

Sadie's eyes gleamed as she topped off his soda. "You'd better be careful," she warned, "or somebody's gonna see that beautiful smile of yours and figure out you're not half as mean and ornery as you pretend to be."

He blinked once, twice, as her comment sunk in. And Sadie made a mental note of the fact that his grin had broadened by the time she closed the door.

"I don't rightly know how long it's been since that boy has cooperated with anyone over the age of twenty-one," Solon admitted as she sat behind her desk. "What are you, some kind of angel?"

She met his dark eyes and hoped he couldn't hear her heart hammering in response to the intensity of his wide-eyed admiration. "You'll find neither halo nor wings on this human, Mr. Turner."

"Solon," he corrected, then quickly added, "seems only fitting, since we're going to be discussing my boy on a regular basis."

All right, so he's handsome and polite, she told herself, *but let's not forget our motto, Sadie old girl. . .* "Mr. Johnson tells me you own a general contracting firm."

He nodded. "Used to build houses. Now I'm into commercial construction, mostly. It's not nearly as satisfying as putting up houses folks call home, but there's good money in it."

"Mmmm, so you're rich *and* successful, too." Immediately, Sadie regretted her little joke, for it had etched a deep furrow on his brow.

"I do all right, I guess, but. . ."

"But the success comes at too high a price?" she finished for him.

Solon pursed his lips and rested his left ankle on his right knee. "You sure don't mince words, do you. . . Miss Burke?"

She knew why he'd paused. He wanted her to invite him to call her Sadie, as he'd invited her to call him Solon. *Well, he can just sit there 'til pigs wear glass slippers,* she told herself. *This is a professional relationship, and that's all it's ever going to be. . .no matter how gorgeous he is!*

As Jesse had done earlier, his father now tucked in one corner of his mouth. "I'll admit, you're nothing like any of the other shrinks I've met."

Considering Jesse's angry attitude and thick file folder, she imagined Solon Turner had no doubt talked with his share of her peers. "I'm not *like* other shrinks because I'm *not* a shrink." She quickly explained that the nickname had been affixed to psychologists and psychiatrists only. She leaned forward, grinned, and raised her left brow. "My granny had a name for folks like me." She squinted her eyes and rounded her shoulders to begin the imitation of her grandmother: "'My girl Sadie,' she'd say, 'is the best wig picker this side of the Rockies!'"

Not even her shenanigans restored the man's smile. "It's been my experience that people in your. . .*profession*. . .seem bound to dig up new problems rather than solve old ones." He'd said *profession* as though it were a vile, criminal activity.

"I won't debate the moral character of those in my field," Sadie said, "because you and I are both old enough to know there are good and bad in every arena of life." She raised one brow. "Why, I'm sure if we looked hard enough, we could find an unethical contractor out there somewhere."

Point well scored, she thought as Solon's eyes widened in

response to her retort. Calmly, she opened the file folder and cleared her throat. "Now, about Jesse. . ."

"Whatever it costs, I'm good for it," he said, withdrawing a brown leather checkbook from his breast pocket.

Sadie chose a blue felt-tip from her pencil cup. "Mr. Johnson didn't explain the. . .ah. . .the *arrangements* with you?"

Solon's brow crinkled with confusion. "He only said the Thornton School would be worth everything it cost me."

She summoned the strength not to laugh out loud. How like her old friend to leave the dirty work to her. *Thanks a heap, Mr. Johnson*, she thought, smiling to herself. Then, sighing, she told Solon, "Maybe I'd better tell you the *rest* of the Thornton story." Leaning back in her chair, she laid the pen on her desk and began.

"Miss Betina Mae Thornton never married, you see, and from a very young age she supported herself by serving Baltimore's rich and famous. . .politicians, writers, entrepreneurs. She lived a very simple life, and invested in what was, at the time, a business phenomenon. People called her crazy for spending her hard-earned dollars on American Telephone and Telegraph stock, but she paid them no mind. She remembered as a little girl hearing her father's voice over the telephone for the first time. 'Sounded like God,' she wrote in her journals.

"She had always been a devout Christian, and even after she retired—at the ripe old age of ninety-five—she spent every Sunday afternoon at the German Children's Home out in Catonsville, working with the orphans.

"I've read all her journals, and the way those children lived just broke her heart, so she decided to do something to ensure that *all* children would be given a chance at a good education and a normal, happy life.

"So one day, without a word to anyone, Betina bought up the last acres out behind Patterson Park, commissioned the buildings and grounds you see here today, and enclosed the entire project behind fancy wrought-iron fences." Sadie propped one elbow on the edge of her desk, leaned her chin on an open palm, and added, "She left strict instructions about who would profit from her investment after she left this old world; there will likely be enough money in the Thornton School account to care for troubled teens long after you and I have joined her in Paradise.

"So you see, Mr. Turner, while we'd never turn down a donation, it's not your money we need. What we do need, if you don't mind the cliches, is your commitment to put your nose to the grindstone and provide us with some elbow grease. Every day, there's something that needs tending around here. . .clogged drains to clear, creaking doors to oil, leaking roofs to patch, lawns to mow, hedges to trim. . .the list goes on and on. We ask that parents give as much time as they can spare—so that the school will have more money to spend on what really counts: the kids. And we want the kids to see that their parents are willing to work, really work, on their behalf."

She picked up the felt-tip pen once more and shot him a lively look. "So, when can you begin?"

Solon, elbows on his knees now, only shook his head. "Right away! I can get you the best maintenance crew money can buy."

Sadie scowled. "I'm not making myself clear, I see. The children already know what money can buy, Mr. Turner. What they need to learn is that people will give of themselves on their behalf."

He stared blankly for a moment, then said, "I. . .I left my appointment book in the car. Can I call you when I get back to the office?"

She slid open her top desk drawer, withdrew a crisp white business card, and handed it to him. *Sadie F. Burke* the first line of raised black script said, *Counselor*. Beneath her name and simple title, the address and phone number of the Betina Thornton School. He tucked it into his checkbook, then returned the checkbook to the inner pocket of his suit jacket.

"So, tell me, how do we proceed from here?"

"Well," she said, standing, "on his first day of school, Jesse will be provided with all the books and supplies he needs. Classes start at eight sharp; school is dismissed at three. Teachers are available before and after school, on a first-come, first-serve basis. But you'll learn the details at your first parent-teacher meeting."

"The first. . ."

Sadie nodded. "It's not a requirement, of course, but parents are encouraged to come in for a counseling session at the beginning and at the end of each week, so they'll be aware what teachers expect from their children—and so we'll know about anything in their personal lives that might affect their work here." She raised her left brow again and gave him a quick once-over. "I can tell you this: The students who come to Thornton seldom have a surplus of parental involvement, but when parents get convinced to get involved, right from the start, the kids are here and gone in no time."

"How many return?"

"In the six years I've been here, I've seen hundreds of kids come back. . ."

Solon's dark eyes widened, and then he frowned deeply.

"To share new successes with old friends," Sadie quickly added.

He smiled at that, and Sadie read the relief in his expression. She'd seen enough parents to know Solon would be involved in Jesse's education. . .and his counseling. Still, she felt it only fair to be as honest with the man as possible.

She walked slowly toward the door, then faced Solon. "I want to warn you, Mr. Turner, that Jesse will likely fight us at first—most of the children who come here do. But there's a lot of good in your boy; Mr. Johnson believes in him, and that's good enough for me."

His expression told her he wasn't so sure. Her heart

always ached for caring, loving parents who felt helpless yet hopeful at a time like this. But this time, though she didn't understand why, the ache went deeper than usual.

"I'm sure that before the first week is up, he'll be in the swing of things." Laying a hand upon his forearm, she smiled up at him reassuringly.

"I hope you're right," Solon said, one hand on the carved glass doorknob. "That boy is my whole life. I love him more than. . ."

When the muscles in his jaw tightened as he attempted to control his quivering lower lip. Sadie withdrew her hand from his arm. "Now, don't you worry. Jesse couldn't be in better hands."

He managed a feeble smile and nodded, then opened the door. "I sure do hope so," he said on the other side of it, "because his whole life is riding on this."

two

The hollow *thoink* of the bouncing basketball was punctuated by a hushed *whisk* as the ball fell through the hoop. "Top that one, Jester!" Rasheed yelled.

Jesse hated the nickname the older boy had given him, but the boy's reputation as a bully kept Jesse from admitting it. He neatly rebounded the ball and quickly dribbled it away from the free-throw line, remembering the warning Troy had given him earlier: "Whatever you do, don't mess with Rasheed Potts; he thinks he's Dennis Rodman or something."

Jesse glanced over at Levi, the frail Jewish kid who still sported evidence of how Rasheed felt about being bested at his favorite sport: The mottled purple and blue-green bruise surrounding his left eye stood out in stark contrast to the redhead's pale, freckled skin. *Well, I don't care* what *he wants*, Jesse complained mentally. *I like to win, too!*

He leapt up, the ball resting on the palm of one hand. Eye level to the basket, he pushed it up and out, and watched it roll off the tips of his fingers. For a dizzying moment, every boy on the court held his breath as the ball careened around the rim, hovered motionless, then dropped through the hoop.

"You li'l weasel!" Rasheed hollered, shaking a fist in the air. "Ain't nobody told you the rules? You ain't supposed to sink 'em."

Jesse caught the ball on its first lazy bounce, tucked it under one arm, and leaned casually against a fencepost, as if Rasheed's size and tone didn't terrify him in the least. "The whole purpose of the game is to sink 'em."

Rasheed furrowed his brow and shoved his fist into the pocket of his drooping knee-length jeans. "Well. . ." He

21

narrowed his eyes, as if considering, for the first time, the reason other boys couldn't play their best game. "What are you, a wise guy or somethin'?"

Jesse shrugged, tucked the ball under his other arm. "No. But I like basketball, and I'm pretty good at it, too." Raising one brow, he challenged, "What's the matter, Rasheed—you afraid to find out I'm better than you?"

The bigger boy sneered and doubled both fists now. "Why, I oughta. . ."

That does it! Jesse thought. *I've had enough of people who are bigger, or older, or who think they're some kind of authority figure, telling me what to do!* Bending his knees, he assumed a boxer's pose and hip-hopped back and forth in front of Rasheed.

The bully's brows rose and his eyes widened. "Why you dancin', fool? I don't hear no music."

"If we're gonna play basketball, we're gonna *play basketball*—fair and square—or we're not gonna play at all."

Rasheed snickered. "'Fair and square?'" he quoted. To the other boys, he said, "He been watchin' *Leave It to Beaver* reruns." The grin vanished when he aimed his next comment at Jesse. "You think you gonna fight me, Jester?"

It was Jesse's turn to narrow his eyes. "My name is *Jesse*. If you call me Jester again, I'll stomp you."

Rasheed stood, blinking with surprise, for a long silent moment. Suddenly, a wide smile replaced his smirk. "Hey, you aw-right, Jesse." He dropped a friendly hand upon his new pal's shoulder. "Yep, you're *aw-right*! We gonna be good friends, you an' me, I can tell."

Levi and Troy stood side by side and watched as Rasheed slid an arm around Jesse's shoulders and led him off the basketball court. "First thing we gonna do," Rasheed was saying, "is get you introduced to the Men."

"What men?" Jesse asked.

"*The* Men. My *boys*, my *family*," the older boy explained. "We can use a hard-case 'blood' like you." Laughing, he landed a playful jab on Jesse's shoulder. "You gonna fit right in, man!"

As they left their team mates, Jesse noticed that Levi's milk-white face had paled even further, and he wondered what reason the boy would have to look so concerned.

As if in answer to his unasked question, he heard the boy's high-pitched nasal whisper, "You think he's gonna join the gang?"

From the corner of his eye, he watched Troy run a hand through his tousled blond curls. "Looks that way," he said, pocketing the hand. "I thought he had more sense."

The chain link fence separated them now, and as Rasheed and Jesse passed, Troy and Levi shook their heads. Levi's blue eyes locked hard on Jesse's dark ones, as if to send a silent warning by way of the intense gaze. Jesse shuddered involuntarily, frowning at the sudden, unexplainable double beat of his heart.

"He's gonna need all the help he can get," he heard Troy say as he and Rasheed rounded the corner. The unmistakable sounds of a bouncing basketball echoed in the courtyard.

"You win some," Levi said as the ball *whooshed* through the hoop, "and you lose some. That's just the way it is."

⋟

"It's come to my attention that you've been hanging around with Rasheed Potts."

Jesse glared at Sadie. "You can make me come to these stupid meetings, and you can make me show up at Thornton every day, but you *can't* pick my friends." *Friends! Rasheed isn't your friend; why are you telling Miss Burke that he is?* He dug his knuckles into his eyes, wondering as he hid in his self-imposed darkness, why he'd spoken to the counselor in such angry tones.

She'd asked him halfway through their very first meeting, two weeks ago today, precisely what he thought was the reason for his surly behavior. And he'd told her, truthfully, that he didn't know. Late that night, Jesse had stared at the dark ceiling above his bed and asked himself why he'd been picking fights with classmates, why he'd skipped school, why he'd given his teachers so much trouble. Why, when in the past he'd looked forward to his father's big bear hugs and 'noogies to the noggin,' now he avoided even being in the same room with the man.

Nothing made sense any more. *When Mama was alive, things made sense.* Getting into trouble and winding up in Thornton hadn't made sense. Sitting here in Miss Burke's tidy office didn't make sense. Certainly, his mother's death hadn't made sense!

"Jesse, it's a good thing I'm not the sensitive type. . ."

Her voice roused him from his reverie. "Huh?"

Sadie, smiling and shaking her head, said, "You looked as if you were a thousand miles away just now." Rising from her chair, she added, "Why don't we just call it a day?" After scribbling something on the chunky calendar on her desk, she took a deep breath. "Same time tomorrow, okay?"

Nodding, Jesse stood, and added one more thing to his quickly growing list of things that made no sense: *You're not going to cry, Jesse Turner. You, the man—you, the man! You're not going to cry!*

Had it been Miss Burke's patient smile that awakened the sob that ached in his throat? Her quiet, sweet voice? Her wide, dark eyes. . .eyes that looked at him in that same understanding, loving way his mother used to look at him?

Jesse left the office without saying good-bye, and closed the door quietly behind him. He ducked down the first hall he came to and tucked himself into the tiny alcove that housed a drinking fountain. There, back pressed against the cool stone wall, he closed his eyes. *Not again!* he thought. *Not again!*

The pictures in his mind were two weeks old, but try as he might, Jesse couldn't blink them away.

❧

When Rasheed had opened the door to escort Jesse inside,

two fat rats scurried to avoid the bright shard of light that had slipped in through the opening. They disappeared beneath discarded tin cans and wads of newspaper that littered the shadowy hallway.

From one of the upper floors, a baby cried—not a healthy cry, as he'd heard in TV commercials and in the movies—but a weak, pitiful wail, and he wondered what would make an infant sound like that.

Behind the door on the first floor, the bellows of an enraged man mingled with the unmistakable sounds of fists pummeling flesh, followed by the pathetic entreaties of a woman.

"What did you bring me *here* for?" Jesse had whispered, wrinkling his nose as he side-stepped a dead cat. "It smells like a toilet and stale beer." Lurching, he knocked a cockroach from his sleeve. "There's bugs an' rats an'. . ."

In the dim light of the bare overhead bulb, Rasheed's sneer intensified. "What are you, a prissy li'l mama's boy or somethin'? Them rats is more scared of you than you is of them." Touching the tip of his forefinger to the pad of his thumb, he flicked another roach from Jesse's shoulder. "Them li'l ole bugs ain't gonna do you no harm."

Shuddering involuntarily, Jesse did a quick about-face and headed for the door. "I'm leaving, and you can't. . ."

Rasheed grabbed his sleeve. "Okay, okay. Don't get your neck hairs bristlin'. You can leave any time you say. Just come with me, first." He shoved open the door at the end of the hall, and stood grinning in its entry. "I think you gonna be surprised. . ."

Curiosity propelled Jesse forward. Inside, his gaze travelled from ceiling to floor, from wall to wall as he stood stunned into speechlessness by the grandeur of the apartment's interior.

"Welcome to my humble abode," Rasheed said, closing the door.

Plush gray carpeting covered every square inch of the floors, and brightly colored paintings adorned the white walls. White leather sofas and matching easy chairs stood amid brass and glass tables, upon which sat black halogen lamps that lit the space.

"I don't get it," Jesse said, turning a slow circle in his inspection. "How'd this happen. . .*here*?"

Rasheed ran the thumb of his left hand back and forth across its fingertips. "Scratch, man. You can have anything . . .if you have enough scratch."

Jesse frowned. "But why would you want to put all this nice stuff into a building that's condemned. . .or ought to be?"

The boy shrugged. "Rent's cheap." He grinned, then laughed. "Can't beat *free*, now can you?" He pocketed both hands. "So, what do you think of the place? Mighty fine, eh? Migh-tee fi-ine. . ."

Well, there was no denying *that*. The apartment looked like something he might see in one of the decorating magazines his mother used to read. "It's real nice." Then, "You live here. . .alone?"

"'Deed I do," Rasheed answered proudly, lifting his chin. "My daddy took off for parts unknown when I was 'bout seven; only time I see my mama is when she needs money."

"When she needs money, she comes to *you*?" Jesse tucked in one corner of his mouth. "It's the other way around at my house. . ." He thought of his father's famous saying: "Nothing in life is free, Jess; anything worth having is worth working for."

Rasheed's superior smirk faded. Jutting out his lower lip in a childlike pout, he said, "She a crack-head. Been hooked on the stuff for years." He shrugged off the admission, lifted his chin to state, "Don't matter none to me. I do fine on my own."

"But. . .how can you afford all this?"

He wiggled his brows and made the "money in hand" gesture again. "I got my ways."

Jesse scowled. *If he tells me he sells drugs, I'm out of here!* Still, curiosity prompted him to ask, "What ways?"

Rasheed walked into the kitchen and flipped on the overhead

light, flooding the room with bright fluorescence. The black-and-white ceramic tiled floor gleamed, as did the polished white tiles of the countertops. Shining stainless steel appliances glowed with warm reflected light as he opened the refrigerator. "Beer? Wine? Soda?" he asked, poking his head into the well-stocked shelves.

"Nothing for me, thanks," Jesse said from his side of the bar counter. "You really live here all by yourself?"

Something glowed in Rasheed's eyes when he said, "I said I did, didn't I?" and Jesse couldn't decide if that something was pride or sadness or loneliness.

Just as curiosity had propelled him here in the first place, it made him ask, "So what do you do for all this. . .," he mimicked the hand gesture, ". . .scratch?"

With his shoulder, Rasheed shoved the refrigerator door shut. "Drugs." Emptying a can of Coor's into the glass tumbler he'd taken from the drainboard, he shrugged. "What else?"

Now Jesse understood why Levi and Troy had behaved so peculiarly when Rasheed led him away. They knew all this and feared for Jesse's well-being. He glanced at his watch, prepared to fabricate a reason to leave, when the door burst open and three boys came into the room. Jesse needed no introduction to know these were the Men.

The biggest stood no less than six feet tall and wore a tight-bound blue bandanna around his head. His grimy white T-shirt said, *STUPID*. Beside him, a curly-haired Hispanic twirled the stud in his nose as he flapped an identical bandanna hanging from his jeans pocket. His T-shirt said *I'M WITH STUPID*. They were holding up a third boy. . .a smallish kid in high-topped sneakers who had knotted two blue bandannas together and used them to hold up his baggy shorts. "Chubby, here, ain't doin' so hot," said Stupid.

"Too much of a good thing," I'm With Stupid added.

Rasheed shook his head. "He never did know when to quit, did he?"

Jesse's heart hammered. *Shouldn't someone call 911?* he wondered.

A thread of drool oozed from the unconscious boy's mouth, down his chin, puddling on his sizeable gut. His dark lids fluttered open now and then, exposing eyeballs that appeared to be trying to study his own brain. And then Jesse saw the trail of blood that dripped steadily from the crook of his arm onto the silvery carpeting. . . .

Rasheed saw it at the same time. "Aw, would you look at that!" he yelled. "He's bleedin' all over my rug. Hand me that towel, there," he ordered Jesse. "Hey, Mohammed, get that old cleaning lady in here 'fore he stains my stuff."

Jesse tossed the towel, refusing to get any closer to the Men than necessary. "Lay him down on the kitchen floor," Rasheed barked, pressing the towel against the bloody hole in the kid's arm. They worked swiftly and efficiently, making it obvious they'd done this before, and in a matter of minutes, they had the bleeding stopped.

As they bent over their slowly recovering friend, Jesse slipped out of the apartment, raced down the stairs, and burst through the door. When the cold, sunny February air hit him, he thought he knew how it would feel to be deep underwater when your oxygen tank ran dry. He leaned against a parked car for a moment, gulping the breeze as a man too long in the desert might quench his desperate thirst.

He looked up at the windows of Rasheed's elegantly furnished apartment and fought the urge to retch. And then he ran, full out, until the familiar and welcoming sight of his own house came into view.

ૐ

"Jesse Turner, what are you doing out of class?"

Mr. Miller, Thornton's aging shop teacher, roused him from his memory. "I was just in with Miss Burke," Jesse explained, stepping away from the water fountain.

"Get on to your next class then," the old man said, eyeing the boy suspiciously. "You need a late pass?"

Jesse glanced at his wristwatch. Sadie had let him leave early; he still had ten minutes before his next class began. "No, thanks, Mr. Miller," he said as he headed down the hall. *Wish there was some sort of old pass that would get me free of Rasheed,* he thought.

⋆

"I hate it here," he complained to Sadie the next morning. "You people treat us like we're a bunch of retards or something. . .all this group therapy and one-on-one counseling." He glared openly at her. "I'm *not* crazy!"

"No one ever said you were, Jess," she said softly.

"See? That's just what I mean!" He threw his hands into the air.

Sadie frowned. "I'm afraid I don't know what you're talking about."

"You talk to me like I'm some kind of half-wit, or. . .or. . . some kind of *baby* or something." He folded his arms over his chest. "I *hate* it here!"

She lifted one brow and took her time responding to the angry youth. "Did you ever stop to consider maybe it's because you reap what you sow?"

He aimed sullen, hooded eyes at her. "Oh, great. So now you're gonna quote the Bible at me." Exasperated, he expelled a mouthful of air. "You people are good at spewing out that God stuff, but you never explain it."

Sadie sat on the corner of her desk. "'You people'? Just exactly who are 'you people'?"

Jesse looked thoroughly disgusted now. "Grown-ups, who else!" he barked. "You, my father, Mr. Johnson. . .all you people ever want to do is talk the talk. Not one of you ever wants to walk the walk."

Sadie's brows drew together.

"On the street," he said, rolling his eyes, "I'd better walk the walk, or," he added in a singsong voice, "'sticks and stones *will* break my bones, and talk will never save me'. . . even fine talk from a true lady like you, Miss Burke." He tucked in one corner of his mouth and rocked his head from side to side, and mouthed a silent *"Duh. . ."*

Sadie laughed softly. "Well, on behalf of all the lecturing adults in the world, I apologize. And let me be the first to explain what *this* lecture, at least, means."

She stood and planted both fists on her hips. "'You reap what you sow'—I believe that's what I said." One finger to her lips, she squinted and nodded. Then, "If you're a farmer, and you plant wheat in your field, what is going to grow?"

Jesse mugged a dim-witted expression. "Uh. . .uh. . . wheat?"

Ignoring his sarcasm, she continued in a light voice. "That's right. If you *sow* wheat, you'll *reap* wheat." Without warning, she whirled around to face him and leaned her palms on the arms of his chair. "And if you plant lies, violence, and bitterness in your heart," she hissed, "what do you suppose is going to grow *there*?"

He hadn't expected the nose-to-nose confrontation, and pulled back as far as the chair back would allow. Just as quickly, his tough-guy facade returned, and he faked a small, timid voice. "I. . .uh. . .more of the same, Miss Burke?"

She'd been working with this kid for days now, and she hadn't seen a glimmer of hope that she'd even begun to reach him. He reminded her of White Fang, the half-dog, half-wolf in Jack London's classic tale.

Sadie had but one tool with which to unlock this stubborn boy's heart: patience. She straightened and went around to sit behind her desk. "You know, Jess, I've learned that no matter what color our skin, no matter how old or young we are, no matter how smart. . .or how *stupid*," she added, emphasizing the word, "how rich or poor, human beings have a lot of things in common. And one of those things is the need to be accepted, to be liked, to have friends."

He sighed, as if to say, *Yeah, and what's that got to do with anything?*

"When I was in college," she continued, refusing to allow

his bitter attitude to control the session, "I knew a boy who had hundreds of friends on campus."

Though he refused to look up, Sadie could tell he was paying attention by the way his expressive face reacted to her words. His brows rose when her tone did, and they lowered when her voice grew soft.

"On the weekends," she went on, "Buddy played drums in a rock band. Do you know what was painted on his bass drum?"

Jesse rolled his eyes. "What?"

She leaned forward. "He painted the message himself."

He met her eyes to bite out, "So, what did his drum say, already?"

Grinning, she pointed her finger at him. "'Nobody likes a smart aleck,'" the fingertip scribbled on the invisible blackboard between them. "It was Buddy's life motto and, I believe, the reason everybody loved him."

She rolled the desk chair back and stood. With a wave of her hand, she showed him the door. And just before he pulled it closed behind him, she said, "Think about *that* before you meet me here again, same time, tomorrow."

⁂

His father had obviously left work early to get home and put on the pot of spaghetti sauce. The thick, spicy aroma of it hit him in the face like a warm barber's towel the moment he opened the front door.

"Hey, Jess. You're home early. . .How was school today?" Solon called from the kitchen.

"Fine." He didn't want to talk about school. Didn't want to talk about Buddy the drummer, or reaping what he sowed, or Rasheed's gang, either. Jesse was tired of having everyone else tell him what to do. . .

"How'd the session with Miss Burke go?" came the deep, raspy voice.

"Fine."

He'd just flung his book bag into the hall closet and was

about to head upstairs to his room when Solon appeared in the foyer, drying the soup ladle with a red-checked dish towel. "Made your favorite for supper."

Jesse knew that smile. . .It was the forced, unnatural grin that told him his father meant something different from what his words were saying. Jesse took a deep breath. He didn't know what his father was thinking anymore. Jesse wished he would just leave him alone, instead of asking things like, "Why are you so angry, son?" and "What are you angry *about*?" Because the plain truth was, Jesse didn't *know*!

"Sauce smells great," he said, mirroring his dad's grin.

"Why don't you go on upstairs and get washed up while I set the table?"

Thankfully—and Jesse climbed the wide staircase, his palm sliding up the polished mahogany banister as he went. Ever since he was a boy, he'd loved the feel of the cool wood that curved gracefully from the foyer to the first floor landing. Loved listening to his hushed footfalls, too, as his sneakered feet landed on each plush-carpeted step.

As always, he walked quickly past the huge, sunny room that had been his parents'. . .before cancer took his mother. Avoiding that room was something he and his father had had in common, right from the get-go.

After Coral's funeral, Solon had emptied his bureau drawers, closet, and chiffarobe, and made dozens of trips back and forth to the room across the hall. There, he filled the dresser and the closet—reserved for overnight guests' clothes—with his own pants and shirts and shoes. From that night on, he slept in the smaller room, saying the double mattress offered more support to his back than the queen-sized bed he'd shared with his beloved Coral. . .

Sometimes Jesse thought his mother's presence still filled the high-ceilinged house. If he stood quietly in the living room, he could almost hear her, humming softly as she dusted the bookshelves flanking the flagstone fireplace. If he closed his eyes in the kitchen, he could almost inhale the scent of steaming chocolate chip cookies, fresh from the oven. If he stared long enough at the portrait that hung above the mantel—the one Solon had commissioned as a surprise anniversary gift the year before the diagnosis—he could almost see her beautiful, full-lipped smile pull back in that teasing grin. But his dad never seemed to sense her presence the way Jesse did; in fact, he seemed to have forgotten all about Jesse's mom. He never talked about her, never put up any photos of her around the house, never even went to her grave anymore.

A week after they'd buried her, Jesse had scoured the house, gathering every snapshot he could find, and dumped them in the middle of his bed. He had taken hours to find what he'd been searching for, and when he did, he'd stuffed the rest of the photographs into a boot box and shoved it into the back of his closet, where it had remained to this day. He'd emptied his bank, then, and hiked down to the mall, where he bought a silver frame.

Now, sitting at his desk, Jesse picked the picture up and stared at the magical smile that could sweeten even the most sour mood. "Oh, Mama," he said softly, blinking back hot tears, "things aren't the same without you."

Ever so gently, he returned the silver-framed photo to the nightstand and lay down to stare at it. "I guess you know I started a new school. It's not such a bad place, really, but. . ."

"Jesse," Solon called from the bottom of the stairs. "Supper's ready."

Jesse sat up, knuckled his eyes, and sniffed. "Be right down," he hollered. "I'm just gonna wash my face. . ."

As he headed for the bathroom down the hall, Jesse paused in his doorway, glanced back at the snapshot and whispered, "I sure do miss you. . ."

જ

"I can't believe you just picked up the phone and called him!"

Hannah shoved the sugar bowl closer to her sister, then sat

across the kitchen table from her and stirred her own cup of tea. "Well, not everybody is as shy and reserved as you are, little sister."

"So what did he say when you told him who you were?"

Like a blushing schoolgirl, Hannah hid behind her hands. "He said, 'You're pulling my leg; this isn't Hannah Burke . . .the li'l gal who used to tattle on me every Sunday for pelting her with paper airplanes. . .'" Peeking between two fingers, she added, "And I said, 'Yep, it's me; one and the same.'"

Sadie sighed and rolled her eyes. "Just skip to the part where he invited you to dinner at the Peabody. . ."

Hannah squealed with delight and clasped both hands under her chin, reminding Sadie of days long gone, when she and her older sister would sit cross-legged in the middle of matching twin beds, whispering—when they should have been sleeping—about good-looking boys and church socials, lipstick and nail polish, homework and housework and high-heeled shoes.

"Seems our mama told *his* mama that Calvin ran off and left me to raise two young'uns all by myself. He said he admired me. Said 'Lots of women in your shoes might have fallen flat on their faces. Not Miss Hannah Burke!' he said. 'No siree!' he said, 'Hannah Burke, she went back to school and got her degree, and found a job teaching so she could put a roof over her kids' heads.'"

Hannah grasped Sadie's forearm. "He said he *respected* me. Can you believe it? Said if there were more sisters like me in this ole world, men like Calvin would cease to exist, 'cause they'd be too *ashamed* to run off and leave their women and children!"

Sadie smiled fondly at Hannah. "Floyd isn't the only one who respects and admires you." Their gazes locked for a moment before she added, "Why, you're my hero. . . 'specially now that you've gone and got all snooty on me. . . eating at the Peabody and all," Sadie gushed.

"Oh, go on with you," Hannah said, sending her sister a sideways grin.

"So when are you going to the Peabody?"

She fluttered her eyelashes. "On Friday night. . .right after we attend the symphony. . ."

"The Baltimore Symphony Orchestra? Oh, Hannah," she said, grasping her sister's hands, "I'm so jealous!"

Suddenly, Hannah's delighted expression faded. "Goodness gracious sakes alive, Sadie," she whimpered, hooking eight fingertips over her bottom teeth, "what am I gonna *wear?*"

"Calm down, sister dear." Standing, Sadie held out her hand. "Let's go upstairs and see what's hanging in your closet." With her fingertip, she pushed up the end of her nose and said in a falsetto British accent, "I'm absolutely shoo-ah there is *something* appropriate in your *chiffarobe* for a propah dinnah at the *Pea*-buddy. . ."

Hannah giggled. "Silly goose," she said. Then, bending into a sprint position, she grinned wickedly. "Last one there's a rotten egg!" Hannah dashed for the steps.

"No fair!" Sadie protested, laughing despite the ugly memory the comment conjured. "You cheated!"

Half an hour later, nearly every article of clothing Hannah owned lay in a rumpled heap in the middle of her bed. She crumpled to the floor and buried her face in her hands. "I'll have to call him back and cancel." Her moist eyes met Sadie's. "What are the chances a man like that will fall for a gal whose wardrobe is more suited to eat at McDonald's than to dine at the Peabody?"

Sadie sat beside her and sandwiched Hannah's hands between her own. "Sounds to me like he's grown up into a good and decent man. I'm sure he'll understand. . ." But even as she said the words, Sadie's brain was cooking up an idea. Hannah would turn thirty-five next month; surely her sister wouldn't mind opening her birthday gift a little early. . .

"Well, I've got to get home. I have a ton of work to do around the house before I go over my files for tomorrow's sessions." She got to her feet, held out her hands, and helped Hannah to hers. "I've got this new kid. . .and he's a handful, let me tell you. I'm probably going to end up on a wig picker's couch myself before I get his punkin head straightened out!"

"Whoever the little bugger is," Hannah began, "his luckiest day was when he met my sister." She gave Sadie a hearty hug. "Go on, then. Leave me alone to wallow in self-pity, in a pile of frumpy duds that a bag lady would be ashamed to wear."

Sadie grinned, knowing she'd make a stop at the Hecht Company on her way home to check out the dresses in their ladies' department. She'd seen enough of her sister's things just now to know exactly what size to buy. By this time tomorrow, Hannah would have an outfit to wear to the Peabody that would knock the fancy Italian leather loafers clean off Floyd Barnes's lawyer feet!

"I'll call you first thing tomorrow," Sadie said, bussing Hannah's cheek with a light kiss. "Maybe we can 'do lunch.'" She glanced at the pile of clothes on the bed. "Have fun putting all that back where it came from," she added, then dashed down the stairs.

&

Sadie turned down the volume on the car's radio, effectively silencing WJHU's Mark Steiner Show. *Whoever the little bugger is,* Hannah had said, *his luckiest day was when he met my sister.* From all outward appearances, Sadie admitted, Jesse Turner hadn't had a lucky day in a long, long time. And neither had his father, thanks to the boy's surly disposition.

She pictured Solon Turner's slanted, brooding brown eyes. The man had only smiled once or twice in all the times she'd seen him. . .and she'd seen him on many occasions now, what with their three-way counseling sessions with Jesse and their one-on-one chats about the boy. And while the smiles did a lot to enhance his already handsome face, they never quite reached his haunted eyes.

She acknowledged that Coral Turner had touched her husband and son in ways few others could. . .or likely would. When she was alive, Art Johnson had told her, Solon and Jesse seemed likely to stand the world on its ear. Without her, these strong, handsome males had lost that strength. *Oh, to be loved like that,* she mused.

Love sure is a funny thing, she thought as she wheeled her Mustang into an empty parking space in the mall lot. *It can make the world go round. . .or stop it spinning altogether.*

Sadie locked the car with a sure hand, much in the same way she'd locked her heart after Evan left her at the altar. It had been, by far, the most humiliating experience of her life to be left standing, alone and trembling, in the little room near the vestibule, while the church pews filled up with friends, neighbors, co-workers, and relatives.

She had heard them chattering in hushed tones as she checked and rechecked her hair and makeup, looked time and again to ensure her billowing petticoats weren't showing past the hem of her flouncing gown, and adjusted her veil, her gloves, the velvety white roses in her bridal bouquet.

At precisely two o'clock, the voices had dimmed when Mrs. Jones started her off-key rendition of "Here Comes the Bride." The old woman played it six times before turning to another page in her tattered, battered songbook. She banged the yellowing organ keys as if she were doing a Jerry Lee Lewis impression, issuing a barely recognizable version of "Now Joined By God" through the instrument's gleaming pipes. "Wherever You Go" had come next. Then "How Great Thou Art" and "Faith of Our Fathers."

Evan was, by then, over an hour late. "He's not coming," her pacing, hanky-twisting mother had said. "The good-for-nothing man has stood you up!" *Of course he has,* Sadie had admitted at five past two. But she couldn't say so out loud. Not when a church full of people waited to watch her float down the aisle in a dress of virginal white!

By three o'clock, she'd peeled off her elbow-length gloves and tossed her filmy beaded veil across the room. *He didn't even bother to send a note or a friend with a message!* she'd ranted.

What *could* she have done but dry her tears, and her mother's, too, and march down that aisle—alone, and in time to nothing but the music of her hammering heart! She'd stood at the altar and primly folded her hands at her waist. "I'm sure most of you have seen *The Graduate*," she'd said. "There won't be a dramatic 'interrupt the ceremony' scene today," she'd added, the first two fingers of each hand drawing quotation marks in the air, "because Evan made the same point by merely not showing up!"

She'd said it with a bright, brave smile on her face and an upbeat, light tone in her voice. "But I see no reason to cancel the reception, do you?" She'd stepped off the altar to peek at her mother's wristwatch. "The party starts in fifteen minutes." Hitching up her skirts, she'd run back down the white-sheeted aisle. "Last one there's a rotten egg," she hollered, and disappeared into the dressing room to gather her wits. . . and her composure.

She would not walk into that banquet hall red-eyed and stuffy-nosed. . .not for the likes of Evan! Sadie had chosen instead to focus on the positives: Life with a man like that would have been a disaster; better to have found out his true nature now, rather than later. What if he'd decided to leave after they'd had a child or two, the way Hannah's husband Calvin had? Besides, she had plenty to thank God for. . .and she thanked Him every time she accepted the heartfelt sympathies of her wedding guests.

Eventually, the celebration geared up to a full-scale party. And when it all ended in the wee hours of the morning, Sadie admitted, somewhat wistfully, that it had been the first time she'd ever seen guests carrying fancifully decorated packages *away* from a wedding reception. . .

This is the stuff Burke women are made of! she told herself now as she picked through the racks of women's wear at the Hecht's. It was what had allowed her Granny, her mama, and her sister to survive—and succeed—after having handed over their hearts, only to have them battered and broken by undeserving men.

Hopefully, that same stuff would get her past this ridiculous crush she seemed to have developed on Solon Turner, too!

three

Solon had visited the construction site first thing that morning. Last week, he'd scheduled a meeting with the developer to walk him through this, phase two, of the Hunt Club project.

The office complex stood on five acres of prime Howard County real estate. Ten buildings in all—each six stories high and mostly smoked glass—faced one another across a circular parklike expanse of lawns and gardens. When complete, The Grove, as the architect had named it, would boast fountains, a fishpond, and a stream—all fed by an intricate underground water supply system.

Bridges and walkways would wend through the canopy of trees that had likely rooted themselves to this spot centuries ago. Solon had been immovable on that score: None of the ancient oaks, birch, and maples would be destroyed to make space for parking—or anything else, for that matter!

He was hoping the Hunt Club project would get his company on the list of companies nominated for the coveted Best Builder Award. If Turner Construction could land that plaque, his employees could count on a long and secure future. Media coverage had garnered big-bucks deals for companies that had earned the medal in the past—deals that allowed them to open up shop in Washington, D.C., Richmond, New York, Raleigh-Durham. . .Even if he didn't win, he'd be honored just to make the list.

To succeed in this mostly white, male-dominated industry, he'd been told by the Urban League that his chances of making it were slim to none. And he'd responded by saying he saw only two colors: green cash and gold medals. He knew he'd have to prove exactly what *this* black man was capable of doing. Fifteen years after opening the doors to his business, he stood shoulder to shoulder with the biggest names in the country. . .and he'd done it without ever having to say that the white man was holding him down. It hadn't been easy beating that ugly monster called racism, but the whole process had been made easier by dint of his own drive to be recognized for what he could do, instead of the color of his skin.

Solon had hired a head hunting firm, and told the rep he'd pay top dollar for the country's best salesman. He interviewed dozens of men before finding the one who would help him reach his goal. Within five minutes of their first meeting, Solon knew that Michael Joseph Mulhearne would be a smart investment. Sure he was a short white guy—but the two of them thought alike.

"*Michael* sounds too pompous and arrogant," Mr. Mulhearne had said, grinning and winking like a giant leprechaun. "Call me Joey, all my friends do." Solon and Joey had soon formed an unbeatable team. Solon provided the brains that shaped the strategy—and Joey provided the sweet talk that landed them deal after deal.

Solon was proud of what he'd made of Turner Construction. Proud that he'd helped a few brothers get a much-deserved chance at success. If someday he won the Best Builder award, he'd be accepting it as much for their achievements as his own. . .He wanted that award more than just about anything he'd ever wanted in his life.

But not as much as he'd wanted Coral to become his wife.

And not as much as he'd wanted God to spare her when the cancer struck. . .

Not nearly as much as seeing an end to Jesse's problems either. He had a feeling that, just as Joey had been the perfect partner for his business ventures, Sadie Burke would be the individual he needed to help him achieve his son's victory.

As he drove from the project to Thornton, her pretty face with its dancing golden-brown eyes and bright smile flashed in his mind. Her lilting voice warmed him, right to the marrow of his bones. In her presence, he felt powerful. Energized. Young and enthusiastic about life. And he hadn't felt like that since. . .

Since the moment before the doctor had told him in quiet, somber tones that Coral's chances of beating the cancer were nonexistent. The man might as well have clamped vise grips around Solon's heart, shutting off the part of him that loved. He had decided right then and there in the hushed waiting room, like the final punctuation mark on the doctor's deadly diagnosis: *You're never going to love another woman as long as you live.*

He'd focused on the sound of the surgeon's sponge-soled shoe covers, squeak-squeaking back down the waxed linoleum floor of the corridor toward the operating room. When the double doors hissed shut behind him, Solon had slumped into the nearest chair, held his face in his hands, and wept, oblivious to the pitying stares of passersby. His shoulders heaving, tears squeezed between his fingers and were silently soaked up by the orange-and-green industrial carpet.

He didn't know how much time had passed before the sobs subsided. Solon only knew that when he looked up through bleary eyes, the world was no longer the same place. He stood, ashen-faced and truly alone, for at that moment, he was without God in his heart. There, in the tiny waiting room, he ran a trembling hand through his hair and blamed the Creator for sentencing his wife to death.

She'd devoted herself to her parents and his, to him, to their son, toiling tirelessly to see to their every creature comfort. Knowing his father's blood pressure was dangerously high, she had made a point of stopping by twice daily to make sure the old fellow had taken his medicine. Because her own mother's cholesterol bordered on deadly—and the woman had a whole mouthful of sweet teeth—Coral frequently baked healthy yet tasty treats to help the elderly woman resist temptation.

Her house had always been fastidiously clean, her meals

well-balanced and nutritious. She spent Sunday mornings serving meals to the poor in Baltimore's inner city, spent her Friday evenings collecting clothes for the homeless. She taught Sunday school. Sang in the church choir. Volunteered as the "candy lady" at the local hospital. Taught children to read under Mayor Schmoke's anti-illiteracy program. Why had his Coral, this good and decent woman, been stricken with a disease that had been eating away at her like a gluttonous monster?

As he'd contemplated all this, a pair of white shoes had broken into his preoccupation. "Mr. Turner," the nurse had said, "your wife is asking for you."

He'd known he had to pull himself together. Had to be brave and strong, for Coral. He would make her last days as pleasant and pain free as possible. . .

When he stood to head for the recovery room, Solon had caught sight of his reflection in the window encasing the nurses' station. One side of his starched white collar poked out from beneath the maroon sweater Coral had knitted for his last birthday. Earlier, he'd absentmindedly loosened the Windsor knot of his silk tie, and it now hung disheveled and lopsided near his throat. Like a small child dressing himself for the first time, he fumbled ineffectively, trying to straighten the tie and the shirttail that had somehow become untucked.

"Mr. Turner. . . ?"

He'd blinked, then, and swallowed hard. "I'll be right along," he said, his voice deep and foggy with grief. "I just need to splash some cold water on my face."

After sweeping him with an understanding gaze, the nurse nodded. "Of course." Then, "You know the way by now. . ."

Yes, he'd been with Coral through enough surgeries—and enough recoveries—to know where to find her. And yes, he'd be brave and strong, for her, and for Jesse. . .

The thought of his son now roused Solon from his reverie and brought him back to the present. *You're lucky you didn't wrap yourself around a telephone pole*, he admonished himself. *You just drove twenty-five miles in a daze!*

He wheeled the shiny red Ford into a parking space near the school's entrance and glanced at the dashboard clock. *Quarter after nine*, he thought, switching off the ignition. *Fifteen minutes until the meeting with Sadie...*

Solon closed his eyes, hoping to blink away the vision of Sadie's lovely face. He'd made a promise to his wife as she lay dying. "I'll never love anyone as I've loved you," he'd whispered into her ear. "Never..."

Despite the tubes and electrodes attached to her frail frame, Coral had grinned up at him. "You're a sweet man, Solon Turner, but you're a silly man. How can I enjoy heaven if I know you're down here, pining away for me?" The grin faded. "You're barely thirty-five years old, for the love of Sweet Jesus. You have a whole lifetime ahead of you. Of *course* you're going to fall in love again. It's what I've been hoping and praying for ever since I learned that I'd be..."

Her voice trailed off, her jaw clenched, and her small body trembled. The nurse had told him Coral had refused her last dose of morphine. Whether she'd stopped speaking because of the pain of the disease—or because of the pain of saying good-bye—he'd never know. He only knew that what she was saying was nonsense. His age didn't matter one whit. All that mattered was that Coral had been the only woman he'd ever wanted...had ever loved...from the moment he'd first set eyes on her twenty-year-old face at Calvary Church of Christ. How could she think he'd ever be able to replace her...in any way...especially now...

He'd been known as the Miracle Man in his football days, somehow always able to snatch victory from defeat in the last desperate seconds of the game. But the two-minute warning in the fourth quarter had sounded, and he felt helpless, powerless in the face of this overwhelming foe.

"Hush, now," he'd said, patting her hand. "Get some rest, why don't you, while I..."

She'd chosen that moment to look deep into his eyes, and with a clarity he hadn't seen in days, she held his gaze. "It's time, Solon," she rasped, squeezing his hand with a strength that belied her condition. "I just can't take the pain any longer. I want to go home, to Jesus." A lone tear oozed from her eye, leaving a shining trail as it rolled down her cheek. "I'm so sorry, my sweet man, to leave you with so much to do. . ."

"I said 'hush,'" he'd repeated, trying hard to be strong, to staunch the tears that threatened to spill from his eyes. "You hear me? You rest, now, and. . ."

Coral had sighed, shook her head slightly. "There's a whole basket of ironing in the laundry room, and it's half-full of your work shirts. . ." She sighed wearily. "I never got around to weeding the rose garden, or painting Jesse's room. . ."

Even as she lay breathing her last, her concerns had been for him, for their son.

"It hurts so bad, Solon. So very bad. . ."

"I know, Coral. I know. You want me to call the nurse? Maybe she can give you a shot or something. . ."

"No. No, don't do that. I want to be awake, because what I'm going to say is important." She laid her hand atop his then and gave it a slight squeeze. "It hurts bad, but I won't leave. I'll hold on and on until you promise me. . ."

He could see the pain in her eyes, on her lips. She wore it like a badge of honor, but it didn't make watching her suffering any easier to bear. "Anything, honey," he'd said. "Tell me what you want; I'll do anything to ease your suffering. Just please, don't leave me. . ."

She expelled a frustrated, exhausted sigh. "Oh, Solon, please let me go. Don't hold me here, in this world of misery. Please, let me go. . ."

There was no point asking God for help. On his knees, alone in their bed as she lay in the hospital, standing before the altar of the Lord, he'd pleaded for the Almighty's intervention. But no help came. His prayers had fallen on deaf ears, and his sweet Coral withered away, like a lovely cut rose left too long in the sun.

"I don't want to let you go, Coral." He took a deep shuddering breath and continued, "But I don't want to watch you suffer, either." It killed him to say what he did not mean, but he forced himself to say the words she needed to hear. "Go, darlin'. Be with your sweet Jesus. Let go of the pain; Jesse and me, we'll be just fine. I promise. . ."

"You won't turn away when love comes knockin' on your door?"

He frowned as he stared deep into her teary eyes. If he had to lie to make her last moments on earth more bearable, so be it. He wanted to say, *It already came knockin', and when I opened the door and saw you standing there, I knew a love like this wouldn't come calling again.* Instead, he whispered, "All right. . .if it's what you want, I won't turn away."

She closed her eyes then and sighed. "I wish I'd taught you how to use that confounded steam iron. . ." Again her voice had trailed off, and a second shining tear fell from her eye. "Life just ain't fair, is it, darlin'?"

Then, wearing a mere whisper of a smile, she'd left him.

Solon had buried his face in the crook of her neck and tried to ignore the ear-piercing one note of the monitor that, for weeks, had counted her heartbeats with blip after steady blip. "I'll never love another woman as I loved you," he'd repeated, glad she hadn't heard and not knowing or caring whether the dampness on his cheeks had been caused by his tears. . .or Coral's.

Thankfully, a nurse had silenced the monitor's monotonous song. Gently, she laid a hand upon his shoulder. "Your son is on the phone, Mr. Turner."

So he'd sat up. Dried his eyes. And took a last, long look at the love of his life.

Now, as he locked the Explorer, Solon forced Sadie Burke's face from his mind. Forced her laughter from his memory. Forced himself to repress the picture of her smile. "Not now, not ever," he muttered, slamming the car door. "I made a promise, and I aim to keep it."

". . .and we've got to consider ourselves lucky we've made this much headway."

The scene reminded him of the old cliché: "You can't see the forest for the trees." In this case, he couldn't hear the words for the voice. . .

She'd been talking for nearly ten minutes, yet Solon hadn't heard a word. *What's wrong with you, man?* he asked himself. *This is your boy she's talking about. Pay attention!*

He shifted in the chair that was too short-legged for his long, lanky frame, lifted his chin, and pursed his lips, as if the actions could ensure his concentration.

Concentration. That's a joke! he told himself as her tiny hands fluttered around her pretty face, emphasizing, underscoring, downplaying. . .as if she needed any assistance at all to help that beautiful voice make itself heard! Solon thought he could listen to the music of her words for hours on end without ever tiring of it.

Sadie was energy personified. Her enthusiasm contagious. And it was all reflected in her eyes. Those mesmerizing eyes. . .She had the biggest eyes he'd ever seen. So big, in fact, that they put him in mind of those apple-cheeked tots on the jars of baby food he'd bought by the case when Jesse was a baby. The color of cinnamon, they were surrounded by a dense fringe of long, black lashes, and flashed with wit and sparked with intelligence. If eyes were the windows of the soul, Sadie, he believed, was as pure and genuine as a human being could get.

Her cheekbones were high and pronounced, her nose long and narrow, reminding him of the pictures he'd seen of Cherokee princesses and Navajo queens. And her mouth, a delightful natural shade of dusty rose, made him think of the wax lips he'd chosen as a kid from the long glass candy case down at the corner store. He'd discarded those two-for-a-penny kind the moment they'd lost their cherry flavor. But if he were ever so lucky as to get his lips near *those* lips. . .

You've gone and lost your mind, Solon told himself. *Not twenty minutes ago, you vowed to keep her at arm's length, to be true to Coral. . .*

His last words to his wife echoed in his mind, and he adjusted his position in the chair once more. *You only promised not to love another woman as you'd loved Coral,* he said to himself. *You never said you wouldn't appreciate beauty when it stared you straight in the eye. . .*

At that precise moment he realized Sadie was staring him straight in the eye.

"Nice of you to join me," she said, grinning.

Solon felt the heat in his cheeks. He licked his lips. "Sorry. There's a lot going on at work lately, and. . ."

Sadie waved his apology away. "Please. I'm the one who should be apologizing. I do have a tendency to go on and on." Giggling, she added, "My mama says I remind her of a chipmunk, the way I chatter endlessly."

He raised his left brow. "Then you're the loveliest varmint I have ever seen." The moment the words were out of his mouth, Solon cringed. He hadn't consciously been thinking such a thought, so where had it come from?

He watched as a twinkle lightened her red-brown eyes as she studied his face. "Did that Irish partner of yours teach you that line of blarney?" she asked, grinning.

He'd spent three long years alone in the darkness of a self-imposed prison. . .two more before that watching Coral die a slow, grisly death. But with the mere power of her smile, Sadie loosed the bolt that had barred his escape, threw open the door, and invited him out into the sunshine. His heartbeat doubled as he basked in her warmth.

Lord, he prayed, *give me the strength to keep my promise to Coral.*

And it never even occurred to him that he hadn't asked God for anything since that dreadful night. . .not until now.

❧

"Be quiet!" Mohammed hissed, a finger over his lips. "If he hears us, we're as good as dead."

"I didn't say anything," Jesse defended.

"Keep it that way, man." He crouched lower behind the row of cellophane-wrapped cookies. "See that soup pot there?"

Jesse followed Mohammed's gaze and nodded.

"They say there's no telling what kind of meat they put in there. . .cat, dog, *kid*. . ."

"Where would he get a goat in the middle of the city?"

"Not that kind of kid, fool. *Our* kind of kid!"

Jesse tucked in one corner of his mouth and frowned. "Yeah. Right." He'd heard the same story, but he couldn't let on to Mohammed that he was afraid of being minced into soup bits, now could he?

"When I give you the signal, we grab all the stuff we can carry, and run like our feets is on fire," Mohammed instructed.

"What signal?"

Mohammed grimaced. "What am I gonna do with you, boy? You such a retard sometimes." He touched his forefinger to his thumb, forming the okay sign. "*That* signal. *Okay?*"

Jesse nodded. He didn't for the life of him know why he'd let Rasheed talk him into this. He'd been in trouble before, some of it fairly serious—but he'd never tried his hand at stealing. This was to be his acid test, though, his initiation into the Bloods, Rasheed's name for his Men.

Rasheed seemed to have cast some magical spell over him; if the boy gave an order, Jesse seemed unable to do anything but follow it. Why had he agreed to participate in this mini-robbery? This was small time, he tried to tell himself, stealing from an old man. . .Still, he was puzzling over the strange control Rasheed had over him when he saw Mohammed give the sign.

Mohammed darted out from behind the cookie stand and

began jamming his pockets full of anything within his reach. Jesse doubted the boy even *liked* mandarin oranges, yet his tattered backpack now overflowed with cans of them. As for himself, Jesse didn't know what to grab. Noodles? Tea? Canned soup stock? He hadn't yet made a decision. . .when it dawned on him that stealing cookies wasn't worth getting his name on a police blotter.

He stood and defiantly strode toward the doors. "Where you think you goin', man?" Mohammed hissed. "You got work to do."

"I don't want anything to do with this. I'm leaving." He turned, and headed for the exit. Jesse felt a cold, hard pressure at the base of his spine, and he knew instantly it was the barrel of a gun.

"You leavin'," came Mohammed's harsh, raspy whisper, "you leavin' this *earth* if you don't do your share."

Biting back his fear, Jesse said, "Go easy, man. Stay cool. It ain't worth killin' somebody over *cookies*."

Suddenly, a shout rang out, and Jesse winced. "Stop! Thief!"

Mohammed, his eyes wild with fright, whirled around and aimed the gun at the aging Korean shopkeeper. Without a second thought, Jesse wrestled the gun from Mohammed's hand. When it clattered to the floor, Mohammed bent to retrieve it. . .and Jesse gave it a hard kick, sending it skittering to the feet of the angry owner.

"What you do here?" the angry Korean shopkeeper demanded, holding the gun on Jesse and Mohammed. "You come to steal?"

Mohammed bolted, leaving Jesse alone to face the irate man. "You no move," the Korean ordered. "I gonna call porice."

"But I didn't do anything!" Jesse insisted as the man dialed 911 and jabbered a nearly unintelligible address into the phone.

Twice in as many minutes, Jesse had been held at gunpoint. Trembling, he held up his hands.

"Stupid boy!" the man said, hanging up the phone. "You no *rook* rike criminal. Why you try rob honest man?"

Jesse noted that it was no fewer than twenty feet between where he stood and the door; the irate Korean had planted himself between him. . .and freedom.

"You resent Korean because Korean work, work, work. Korean no sell drugs to make money." Eyes blazing, the old man used the gun as a pointer. "Korean stand behind counter when sun go up, still stand behind counter when sun go down." Now he was pointing at Jesse's high-topped sneakers. "Not buy fat shoe." And at his leather jacket. "Not buy skin coat. Buy more for store!"

Again, Jesse glanced at the exit and wondered if he could make it that far without. . .

"Ah, I see you rooking at door." The fury in the little man's voice dimmed. He pursed his lips and narrowed his eyes. "You can reave. . .when you tell policeman what you do."

Jesse's heart pounded against his ribcage. "But. . .but I didn't do anything!" he insisted. *And it's* true, he told himself. *I never even touched any of his stuff.*

The Korean, suddenly calm, shuffled toward the cash register and proceeded to rewind the videotape and reviewed what the security machine had filmed. "I see you no rie to Kim; it show here you no try steal." The old man stared hard at Jesse. "Perhaps you would rike to work here?"

"Work? I don't. . ."

"Ah," the man said, "I see I was right; you are spoiled, razy boy!"

"I'm not lazy!" Jesse protested. "It's just. . .I don't—"

The wail of a squad car interrupted him. Two uniformed officers burst into the store, guns at the ready.

"Sorry," Kim said, "robber get away." Grinning slightly, he added, "You see him running down street when you park po-rice car?"

The officers eyed Jesse warily.

"This my de-rivery boy," Kim explained, bowing. "Tell officer your name." Then, as an aside, he shook his head and said, "Kim cannot say American name to save rife. . ."

The policemen and Kim waited as Jesse, shuffling from one foot to the other, tried to make sense of the scene. "Uh, I'm Jesse. Jesse Turner," he said.

The officers holstered their weapons. "You care to file a report, Mr. Kim?" the tallest asked.

Kim glanced at Jesse, then back to the officers. "No point in that," he snapped. "You never catch bad boys, anyway. Go now," he said, waving them toward the door. "Go help yourself to doughnut and coffee before you go. . ."

"Thanks, but we'll just be on our way," the chubby cop said. "Take care," he added, and then they were gone.

"Why didn't you turn me in?" Jesse wanted to know.

"Why you save Kim's life?" Staring at the youngster, he added, "And why you come in with boy who steal? This boy your friend?"

Shaking his head, Jesse stared at the toes of his sneakers. "No. He's not my friend. But if I rat him out, I'm as good as dead."

Dramatic as it sounded, the shopkeeper had lived in the neighborhood long enough to know the boy's words rang true. A moment of silence passed as Kim considered this. When at last he spoke, it was to say, "If you work here, I not tell father you come in with boy who try steal." The man crossed his arms over his chest and lifted his chin.

Young man faced old, like gunfighters at the OK Corral, waiting and watching to see who'd make the first move. Even as he stood there, fighting this battle of wills, Jesse wondered how his father would feel when he told him he'd taken a job.

≈

"Mr. Johnson, how nice to see you!"

"You're pretty as a picture, as always," he said, "but you make me feel like a dinosaur, calling me 'Mr. Johnson.'" He heaved himself into a too-small chair and grunted. "How old do you have to be before you'll finally call me Art?"

Sadie opened the refrigerator beside her desk. "The usual?"

Art Johnson smacked his lips and rubbed his ample belly. "You mean you keep a special supply of warm, store-brand cola on hand, just for me? Sadie, sweetie, I'm touched."

She handed him a paper cup of the frothy liquid. "So what brings you to Thornton this bleak gray day?"

"A bleak gray subject, I'm afraid."

Sadie held up a hand. "Wait. Don't tell me. Let me guess . . .Jesse Turner."

Johnson swallowed a mouthful of the cola. "Never could put one over on you, could I, Brown Eyes?" The friendly grin disappeared. "So how's he doing?"

Sighing, Sadie ran a hand through her hair. "Well, he's not doing badly, exactly. . .but I can't say that I've made any headway with him, either. . ."

The big man nodded. "I'm not surprised. That's why I'm here." He put his empty cup on the corner of her desk. "Where is the little brat, anyway? I'd like to have a talk with him."

She glanced at her watch, then riffled through a stack of papers on her desk. "I have an appointment with him next period, but he's in history class now. He'll be dismissed any minute. If you hurry, you can catch him. . .room 201."

He was out of his seat and through the door with surprising speed for a man his size. "I'll be back here at twelve o'clock sharp," he said, backing past her secretary's desk, "because I'm here to make good on a promise."

Sadie, grinning with confusion, said "Promise? What promise?"

"Remember. . .I promised to buy you a big, fat, juicy steak if Jesse Turner wasn't standing at attention and saluting the flag inside of two weeks." He shrugged, held his hands out in a helpless gesture. "It's been six. What can I say? When

I'm wrong, I'm wrong."

"Better late than never, Mr. Johnson," she said, though he was halfway down the hall by now. "I mean. . .Art. . ."

four

"This is the fifth bathroom I've cleaned this morning, and every last one of 'em was as dirty as this one." The janitor tugged at his yellow rubber gloves and grabbed a handful of wet paper towels from the basin. "Make no mistake: It ain't the hard work, or where it's done that makes me mad; you *young'uns* make me mad," he hissed, "leaving your messes behind for others to clean up for you. Why, if I'd a done things like this when I was a boy. . ."

Jesse rolled his eyes and sighed. He hadn't left the huge pile of brown paper towels in the sink. He hadn't littered the floor with notebook pages. *Why do all grown-ups think they can take their problems out on us kids?* He wondered.

"You'd think some of you would have a little pride in yourselves, 'stead of behaving like a bunch of zoo animals. I'll bet your mama's fancy bathroom was. . ."

His mother's house had always sparkled, and she'd taken pride in the fact, Jesse remembered. In his mind, his mother was an angel in flowing white robes; how dare this man, in his filthy coveralls, even speak her name! "Listen, *George*," Jesse snapped, "I didn't make this mess. It's not my fault you have a dirty job—don't take it out on me."

George, who'd been stuffing the wet towels into the trash can, straightened slowly and faced Jesse. "What's that you say?" His voice was scarcely a whisper.

Jesse squared his shoulders in defiance against the man's wrath. His father had often told him that he shouldn't judge a man by what he did for a living, but by how much pride he took in the job. *But what's the big deal? Surely he's not proud that he scrubs toilets. . . ?*

The man crossed both arms over his ample chest and studied

Jesse before saying, "You think you're better than me, don't you, boy?"

I'm no filthy janitor, Jesse thought, *and I'm never gonna be a janitor.* . .He met the angry eyes that blazed from George's black face and shrugged, his defiance dimming. "No. . .I don't think I'm *better,* but. . ."

"But *you're* gonna grow up and do something clean an' easy for a living, is that it? You're so all-fired fine that if you work at all, you won't push a broom every day of your life. Am I right?"

Jesse gazed longingly at the door and sighed. *So close, yet so far away,* he thought, *just like in Mr. Kim's shop.* . .

"I've seen you, don't think I haven't, struttin' around the halls with the rest of these delinquents, like some kind of peacock. High-steppin' and smirkin' like you're an important man."

He jabbed his bony forefinger into Jesse's chest and held it there, reminding the boy of the science experiment he'd done in seventh grade, when he'd pinned a butterfly to a mat. . .

"*I'll* tell you what's respectable, boy." He began counting on his fingers: "Making good on your debts. Giving your full ten percent to your church. Being a good neighbor. Working hard and making your own way in this world. Getting a decent education. Obeying the law. Voting in every election. *That's* respectable!"

He paused, then shook his head, as if disgusted with Jesse and everyone of the age group he represented. Seemed like the freedom on the other side of the door was looking good to him, too. . .

George pointed a calloused finger at the boy and took a step nearer. "You think 'cause I wear this nasty old uniform, I'm a big nobody, don't you?"

Jesse raised his brows, as if to say, *If the shoe fits.* . .

"Well, let me tell you a little something about George Green. I don't just clean the Thornton School, I clean high rise office buildings. Doctors' offices. Government rooms.

And a whole passel of kids are doing better today 'cause their daddies work for me."

The boy's eyes widened with surprise.

"That's right; you've seen my truck outside: Green Janitorial Services. I *own* the company—*I'm* the boss." He huffed, then added, "Now, I could be in the office, like some kind of big shot, but I don't believe in asking a man to do what I'm not willing to do myself, so I work right alongside 'em, every day, just as long, and just as hard as they do." He narrowed his eyes. "You want to know *why*, boy?"

Jesse only blinked.

"'Cause my daddy taught me if you want folks to respect you, you've got to earn it!" He narrowed his lips. "You proud to be African-American, boy?"

"Well, sure. 'Course I am."

"'Well, sure. 'Course I am,'" George mocked. "Well, I don't believe you."

Jesse only shook his head.

"If you *were* proud of your race," the man continued, "if you had any pride at all, you'd do everything the good people who run this school tell you to do. You'd get yourself *out* of here, quick as you could, and show other kids like you what can happen when you live by the Golden Rule."

From Jesse's point of view, that door was looking better and better. . .and farther and farther away. . .

"I've seen your kind. Too many times. And I'll tell you something else," George said, turning his back on Jesse to stuff a clean liner into the trash can. "If your mama was alive, she'd be ashamed to have raised a boy up to your age who thought just getting by was good enough."

George slammed the lid back onto the trash can. "This school can help you, boy. And if you had half the sense you were born with, you'd know it!" He tossed the overflowing trash bag out the door, then pointed at the mirror. "It's all polished up, nice and shiny, 'cause I don't believe in doing a job halfway. Take a good, long look at yourself once I'm out of here, and ask yourself how long you can stand to live with a fellow who's satisfied with just getting by?"

He stood in the doorway, his challenge hanging in the air between them. "I know your daddy, boy. Bet you didn't know that, did you? Well, I've worked for him for nearly ten years, now. He's one of the most respected businessmen in Baltimore, and he didn't get that respect with a just-getting-by attitude. Think about *that* while you're looking at that silly haircut of yours. What for you wanna go and be such a bad boy, and hurt that fine man?"

Jesse stared back at the man, and then he burst out, "He doesn't care about me. And he didn't care about my mama, neither, when she died."

George regarded him through narrowed eyes. "How you know he don't care?"

"'Cause he never says nothin' about her, and he never says much to me, either."

The janitor stared out the window above the trash can, then reached out to gather up a lady bug from a branch on the shrub growing outside. "You know what this is, boy?"

"It's a lady bug."

George nodded. "I really care 'bout this li'l ole bug." With that, he dropped the tiny critter onto the floor and mashed it flat with the sole of his boot.

"What'd you do that for?" Jesse demanded. "I thought you said. . ."

"Just 'cause I *said* I care don't mean nothin'. It ain't what you *say*, it's what you *do* that counts." He paused, and stared long and hard at the boy. "Sometimes, the hurt can be so bad that you can't let it show. You hold it inside and you can't tell nobody. Your father is that kind of man, boy. You say he don't care. . .Where'd you eat this mornin'?"

"At home."

"Who bought them silly shoes you wearin'?"

"My dad."

"And why are you *here*, in this good school?"

Jesse didn't answer, for he knew what George wanted him to say.

"It ain't what you *say*," George repeated, "it's what you do." With that, he was gone.

❧

"You're ten minutes late, Jesse." Sadie scanned his file, then met his eyes. "This is the fourth time in a row. . ."

He hung his head. How could he tell her he'd been in the boys' bathroom all this time, thinking about what Kim and George had said? How could he explain that Rasheed's constant pressure to become one of the Bloods had cost him a dozen nights' sleep? "Sorry," he muttered.

She got up and walked over to the door, pulled down the shade, and blotted out the light from the waiting room. "All right, Jess," Sadie announced. "It's time."

He met her eyes. "Time for what?"

"Time to come clean with me." Perching on the corner of her desk, she rested a fist on her hip. "We've met three times a week, an hour at a time, since February." She pointed at the calendar on the wall behind her desk. "It's *April*, Jesse. Don't you know me well enough to trust me by now?"

Jesse shrugged. Took a deep breath. Shook his head. "It isn't about trust."

Sadie rested her chin on a bent forefinger. "Then what's it *about*, Jess? What's eating at you? Talk to me, and maybe together, we can fix whatever is wrong."

He sat up straight and wrapped both long-fingered hands around the ends of his chair arms. "You're a nice lady, Miss Burke, and I like you." Meeting her eyes, he added, "But you can't fix what's wrong."

"You'll never know if you don't tr—"

"You can't bring my mama back," he interrupted. "Not even God can do that!"

Sadie licked her lips and frowned, stood and slowly walked back to her desk. Only then did she meet his eyes. "Have you really asked God to bring her back, Jess?" she asked, her voice whisper soft.

His chin was nearly touching his chest when he said, "Every morning and every night, and every spare minute in between. . ." When he looked up, there were tears in his eyes. "I miss her so much."

"Of course you do."

"Nothing has been the same since. . .since. . ." Shoulders lurching, Jesse hid behind one hand, silently sobbing.

Certainly, this wasn't the first time a child had sat in the chair across from her desk and cried. Tears had flowed over bad report cards, broken hearts, family problems. It wasn't even the first time in Sadie's four years as a social worker that she'd seen a student openly grieve over the death of a parent. But she had never seen a boy look quite this forlorn and alone. Almost from the moment Jesse made his heartfelt confession, Sadie understood that a wounded spirit was the cause of his problems.

Her training had prepared her well to comfort kids whose confidence needed bolstering, who believed themselves to be victims of misunderstanding. But face to face with this heart-broken boy, she knew that nothing she'd learned in any classroom could even begin to provide the consolation he so desperately needed.

Dear Lord, she prayed, *speak to my heart, so I'll know which words will comfort him.* A millisecond passed. Two. And then Sadie sent a silent prayer of thanks heavenward, for she knew now what to do.

"Did you and your mother spend much time together, Jesse?"

Still hiding behind his hand, the boy nodded.

"The two of you talked a lot, then. . ."

Another nod.

Sadie believed she knew something about how the boy felt. Her own father had abandoned her, and what was death if not the ultimate desertion? Jesse had likely endured many of the same suggestions she'd heard as a girl: "You're not the first person to suffer such a tragedy; get over it and get on with your life." In Jesse's case, "Your mother would have wanted you to live life to the fullest" had probably been added to the list of recommended healing tactics. If he'd learned, as she had, that the best way to avoid the useless rhetoric was pretense, he too had hidden his true feelings.

I put myself in Your capable hands, Lord, she prayed. And it was a heartfelt prayer, for Sadie knew that the course she would take could do as much damage as good. Jesse, she believed, stood at a crossroads, and if he went in the wrong direction now, he might take a track from which there was no turning back.

Well, here goes, Lord. . .

She would make him remember his mother—the good things and the bad—and she would not soft-pedal her remarks. "How long did you know that your mother might die?"

Jesse knuckled his eyes and exhaled loudly. He spoke in a hushed monotone. "I came home from school one day and found her in the kitchen. Her eyes were all red and puffy, and she asked me to sit down at the table with her. Then she told me she was sick. Very sick." His brow furrowed and his lips quivered as he struggled not to cry. "I asked her if she would die." He met Sadie's eyes, blinked. "And she took my hands in hers and said, 'I don't know, son. But we're all going to pray, because live or die, the next few years aren't going to be easy. . .'"

Sweet Jesus, she thought, *if I'm ever faced with a situation like that, bless me with the strength of that good woman. . .* "She sounds like a wonderful lady."

"She was," he agreed, nodding. One corner of his mouth turned up in a half-hearted grin.

Sadie smiled a bit and sat back to listen to the boy who seemed pleased—relieved, even—to have an opportunity to talk about his mother.

"My mama didn't look for trouble, but she didn't run from it, either. She didn't make excuses for her own shortcomings, and she didn't have any use for people who did."

"Excuses?"

Jesse's dark eyes beamed with loving pride as he explained. "She took a job when my father was getting his business off the ground, cleaning house for a white woman." Smiling fondly, he wiped the last of the tears from his eyes. "She told us at supper that first day that she'd always thought rich people were, you know, neat and. . .and *classy*."

Sadie waited patiently and quietly, hoping she'd soon figure out what Mrs. Turner's job had to do with her son's present difficulties.

"Mama told us the woman didn't want kids 'cause they would have gotten in her way of seeing the world. And she treated her husband like a lap dog. She pretended to have some sort of disability because she was too lazy to do anything around the house."

The smile was gone. In place of the sadness, an angry, indignant expression darkened his face. And the quiet, calm voice gave way to a grating, steely demeanor. "Why did God let that selfish woman live? She doesn't love nobody but herself. Why did He take my Mama? I miss her so much. . ."

Jesse doubled up both fists and pounded on the chair arms, accenting every word. "I miss her and I need her! So if God had to take someone, why not take *that* woman! Who'd miss a woman like that?"

Sadie held her breath and waited again. . .this time for the Lord's benevolent guidance. *Guide my words,* she prayed again, *let what I say be—*

Just then, Jesse leapt up so quickly the chair toppled over behind him. "I ain't no baby!" he growled.

Sadie stood, too. "Of course you aren't."

Pacing like a caged panther, he said, "But. . .I *cried*."

"Even Jesus cried, Jesse. Tears. . .or the lack of them. . . don't define a man."

He stopped in his tracks. "I never saw my dad cry. Not once."

"Just because you've never seen it doesn't mean he's never—"

Jesse interrupted as though she hadn't spoken at all. "Not at the hospital. Not at the funeral home. Not in the cemetery." He looked away just long enough to wrap his hand around the sparkling glass doorknob. "He put all his stuff in the guest room the day we buried her and never mentioned her again." The handle glittered in the bright fluorescent lighting as he moved it half a turn. "She's gone forever," Jesse said, opening the door, "and he doesn't even miss her. If he loved her, he'd miss her." In the doorway, he added, "Maybe he doesn't love me, either. I wish he was dead." His face was tight with angry hurt. "Then I could do whatever I want without him sticking his nose in my business all the time, pretending it's 'cause he cares." He was silent for a long moment, and then he said, "He didn't care about Mama when she died, and I won't care when he bites it."

⋆

"Didn't expect to see you here," Johnson said, extending his big hand.

"Good to see you, Art," Solon responded, pumping the man's arm, then used his hammer as a pointer and indicated the door frame. "'Loose lips sink ships; loose trammel do 'em in.'"

Johnson chuckled, then said, "I only have one student here at Thornton these days; thought since I'm the reason he's here, I'd pay Jesse a little visit." Grinning, he looked conspiratorially over his shoulder. "Seems he's on to me though; haven't seen hide nor hair of him all morning."

Solon tucked in one corner of his mouth. "The boy does have a knack for making himself scarce."

Johnson gestured toward the bench across the hall. Taking a seat himself, he continued, "I like Jesse, Solon. I think with a little more time in this place, he's gonna be all right."

Solon joined him on the bench. "I hope so." He sighed deeply. "I sure do hope so." Brightening slightly, he added,

"He came home last week and told me he'd found himself a job. Said it was time he started pulling his own weight. Never thought I'd see the day. . ."

Johnson nodded his approval. "Good. Good. It shows he's got spunk, initiative. What sort of work will he be doing?"

"Deliveries, stocking shelves, odds and ends, I imagine. He'll put in ten hours a week at Kim's Grocery down on Presto Street."

For a moment, Art Johnson only stared open-mouthed at Solon. The silent moment was suddenly shattered by a thunderous peal of laughter. Slapping his meaty thigh, the principal said, "Kim's, eh?" Wiping tears of mirth from the corners of his blue eyes, he added, "Well, don't that beat all."

Solon frowned. "Is there. . .is there something wrong with Jesse working for Mr. Kim?"

"Wrong!" The booming laugh bounced around the hall once more. "I should say not! Why, when that old Korean gets through with your son, Jesse's gonna know more about the good old American work ethic than you and me put together!"

He waved away Solon's concern. "Trust me. . .and what's more. . .trust Kim. Jesse will earn every dollar the old miser pays him, and he'll learn the meaning of the word *work*, too." He held up a hand to silence the parent. "Kim's the fairest, most honest man I know." A chuckle interrupted his praise of the grocer. "You ever have trouble getting Jesse to clean his room?"

Solon grinned crookedly at the out-of-the-blue question. "Well, sure. Hasn't every parent?"

"Mowing the lawn?"

"Now that you mention it. . ."

"Doing his homework?"

The father tucked in the other corner of his mouth. "Yeah. We've locked horns on that score a time or two."

Snickering softly, Johnson shook his head. "Well, write up those memories in your best journal handwriting, 'cause you've seen the last of your hard-nosed, lazy, teenage son!"

Solon opened his mouth, as if to ask Johnson to explain himself when the man dropped a heavy hand on his shoulder. "So tell me, Solon, what do you think of Sadie Burke?"

Solon blinked at the quick change of subject matter. He'd been thinking of Sadie when Johnson walked up just now, picturing those sparkling eyes, her smile, that funny giggle . . .Blinking again, he ran a finger around the inside of his collar. "Why, I think she's a fine counselor. . ."

Johnson winked again, elbowed Solon in the ribs. "Pretty li'l thing, isn't she?" He shook his balding head. "You ever hear her sing?" He looked toward the ceiling, shook his head some more. "She was born with the voice of an angel, that one. Why, I could listen to it for days. . ." Drawing himself up taller, he added, "She's quite an artist, too."

"Is that so?" Solon raised one brow. He'd known Art Johnson since college, but the man had never tried to line him up with a date before. . .but this was starting to sound suspiciously like matchmaking.

"Yep. That's so. In fact, she's good enough to get paid for her paintings and sketches." He met Solon's eyes. "She's a dandy cook, too. Bet you didn't know that, did you?"

Solon glanced at his watch. "No, I di—"

"She whipped me up a pot of chili once, when I was off work with a head cold." Grinning wickedly, he winked again. "Cleared me right up, I tell you."

"Art. . .I've been widowed long enough to have heard this particular speech before." Solon held up a hand to forestall Art's defense. "Now, don't get me wrong; I appreciate what you're trying to do here. . .and why." He turned slightly on the bench and met the man's eyes directly. "But in all honesty, even if I were in the market for a relationship. . . and I most definitely am not. . .Sadie Burke is my son's social worker. I've always contended that it's foolhardy to mix business with pleasure. . ."

Johnson continued to grin. He slipped his arm around

Solon's shoulders and gave him a fatherly, sideways hug. "She's a good woman, Solon. Got a heart of gold, that one."

"I'm sure she does, but. . ."

Before Solon could object further, Johnson launched into a brief recitation of how Sadie had been left at the altar. . .and how admirably she'd handled the humiliating ordeal. "I wanted to wring that polecat's neck. . .Evan Maxwell, good to the last drip," he said, scowling as he flexed both powerful fists. He shrugged. "Got me two fine, strapping young sons, but never had me any daughters. I'll tell you this, though," he said quietly. "I couldn't love that girl more if she were my own flesh and blood."

The big man rose and headed down the hall toward Sadie's office. "I know these last years have been tough on you. All the more reason you've got to give yourself a life back. Solon, you're the greatest passer the University of Maryland ever had." He winked. "Take my advice and throw a pass Sadie's way. You could do a lot worse."

Standing outside Sadie's office door, he added, "Didn't figure you for a fool, Solon." He put one hand on the doorknob. "But if you don't get to know her better, that's exactly what you are."

Solon's jaw sagged in stunned response to Johnson's last statement. He too stood and faced the direction the principal had gone. "No wonder you're such good pals," he said under his breath. "Neither one of you minces words!"

❧

"Oh, Hannah, I'm so sorry. . ."

"Don't be." Sadie's sister lifted her chin in proud defiance. "If he hadn't done it, I'd likely have been forced to do it myself."

Slipping an arm around Hannah, Sadie frowned. "Now, you know that tough talk of yours is a lot of nonsense. Calvin's been gone for years, and you've never even *tried* to put an end to your charade of a marriage. You believed what you said at God's altar."

Hannah tucked the official-looking document back into her purse and took a deep breath. "I suppose you're right." She squared her shoulders. "But what's done is done."

"You think he'll start visiting the kids and making child support payments now that things are. . .legal?"

Her sister tilted back her head and laughed. "You looking to become the next Eddie Murphy? That's the funniest thing I've heard since that brother left *Saturday Night Live!*"

"Well, stranger things have happened. . ."

Hannah seemed to want no more discussion about her divorce. She whirled around to show off the outfit Sadie had bought her. "So what do you think? Am I a vision of loveliness, or what?"

The suit was indeed stunning, from its mandarin collar to the feminine frog closures that lined the jacket's front. "You look gorgeous in pale yellow, Hannah." Winking, she nodded at her sister's purse, which held the ominous divorce degree. "Good thing that was delivered today—the minute Floyd gets an eyeful of you, he's liable to pop the question!"

They were giggling over that when the door opened and Shirley stuck her head in to announce Art Johnson. In a moment his considerable bulk filled the room. "Good afternoon, ladies," he said, faking a horrible British accent. "What a delightful surprise to find the both of you here, at one and the same time. To what do I owe the pleasure?"

"I have a few errands to run," Hannah explained, standing on tiptoe to press a kiss to the big man's cheek, "and then I'm off to the Peabody in my new party suit!"

"That's right," Sadie interjected. "Our girl has a date!"

Hiding a grin, her sister frowned. "I know it's big news. Why not call Channel 13?"

Sadie ignored Hannah's fake tirade. Holding a hand beside her mouth, she whispered, "Floyd Barnes."

Johnson's eyes widened as he looked from one sister to the other. "Not the hoity-toity uptown lawyer!"

"One and the same."

"The pair of you are beginning to rile me," Hannah announced, narrowing her carefully mascaraed eyes. "I don't have to stand here and take this abuse." She grinned. "I'm leaving, and I have a good mind not to call you tomorrow and tell you a single detail about my once-in-a-decade date!" Wiggling her brows, she flashed a winning smile, then slammed the door behind her.

"I haven't seen her look that happy in years," Johnson observed. "Not that she's had much reason, working hard as she's had to since that rat Calvin deserted her. . ."

Sadie nodded her agreement. "Her divorce papers were delivered today."

The big man grimaced. "You don't mean to say he had the gall to. . . ?"

Again, Sadie nodded.

"Well," he said, dusting his hands of imaginary grit, "good riddance to bad rubbish, I say. She deserves a fellow like Floyd Barnes." He narrowed his sparkling blue eyes and shook a fist in the air. "And if he doesn't treat her like gold, I'll melt him down and make a doorstop outta him!"

Giggling, she grabbed her purse. "My mouth has been watering all morning, thinking about that steak you promised me. Are you ready, Mr. John—I mean—Art?"

He stuck out his elbow. "Porterhouse or T-bone?"

"Filet mignon, I think, and a baked potato overflowing with sour cream, and a spinach salad. . ."

"Do you mind if we stop by the bank on the way?"

"The bank?"

"If you're half as hungry as you sound, I'm going to need to make a withdrawal." Art offered his arm.

Laughing, she took it. They walked down the hall, and passed a silent, surprised Solon Turner on the way. "Good to see you, Solon," she told him.

Solon only nodded, his hammer poised above his work.

"What was *that* expression all about?" she whispered once they were safe in Art's pickup truck.

Johnson chuckled and shifted into reverse. "What do you think of him, Brown Eyes?" he asked, backing out of the parking space.

Sadie clicked her seat belt into place. "He seems like a dedicated parent."

Johnson signaled, then turned left. "I asked what you think of *him*."

She looked at his narrow-nosed profile. "You mean. . .as a *man*?"

Snickering, the principal said, "Uh-huh. As a *man*."

Sadie rolled her eyes. "Well. . .I. . ." She fumbled with her purse straps and stared out the passenger window. "He. . . um. . ."

Of course, she thought he was a good father. And from what she'd witnessed in the months he'd been helping out at Thornton, he was also a talented carpenter. Certainly, she couldn't deny that every female head turned when he walked down the school halls. *He's so. . .cute!*

She'd been so lost in thought, Sadie honestly didn't know if her last thought had been just that. . .or if she'd mistakenly spoken the words aloud. She glanced at Art Johnson, former principal, now co-worker and friend, and studied the rugged face she'd grown so fond of. Seeing not even a hint of a grin, she breathed a sigh of relief. If he'd heard her admission, she'd be the target of a dozen juvenile one-liners about hearts and flowers and other love-related stuff. Still. . .the smile lines beside his eyes had deepened slightly. . .

Sadie slapped a hand over her mouth, just in case.

five

"Mr. Turner, it's Sadie Burke. . .from the Thornton School?"

Solon grinned into the phone. *As if she needs to remind me who she is,* he thought, chuckling under his breath. *I'd have known that voice anywhere. . .*

"Mr. Turner. . .are you there?"

She'd caught him mind-wandering. . .again. Gripping the receiver tighter, he cleared his throat. "Oh. Sorry. What can I do for you?"

He listened to a long pause before she said, "I met with Jesse yesterday, and. . .and I think it's important we discuss him as soon as possible."

Solon glanced at his watch—two-thirty—then at his calendar—two meetings and a visit to the Hunt Club construction site. "This afternoon?"

"Right now, if you can spare the time."

He hadn't known her all that long, but he recognized the tone in her voice. It told him that whatever she had to say about Jesse was indeed important, and if he didn't make the time to talk about it. . .

"I've already taken the liberty of rearranging my afternoon sessions, Mr. Turner. . ."

Tucking in one corner of his mouth, Solon heaved a sigh. "I'll be right over." Joey would have to run both meetings alone, and Solon would check on the Hunt Club's progress tomorrow. "If there isn't a tie-up on 695, I should be in your office in half an hour."

In the silence that followed his commitment, he could almost picture her considering what he'd said. "Let's assume the traffic will be as snarled up as usual—what with all the Beltway construction and the constant fender-benders it

70

causes—and say I'll expect to see you at three-thirty."

"Three-thirty, then," he said, and depressed the hang-up button. In the next five minutes, he rescheduled one meeting, put Joey in charge of the other, and informed the Hunt Club foreman that he'd see him first thing in the morning.

Sadie's secretary was nowhere to be seen when he arrived. Shirley's desk clock said 3:05. He'd made good time. Very good time. Solon sent a silent prayer of thanks heavenward that he hadn't been involved in one of those fender-benders Sadie had mentioned. 3:06 now. *Well,* she said *she'd cleared her calendar for this meeting. . .*Solon walked purposefully toward her door and knocked softly.

"Come in."

The top of her curly-haired head was barely visible behind the stacks of file folders surrounding her. She barely looked up from whatever she was scribbling on the top file to say, "I'll be right with you."

"Sorry I'm so early," he said, taking a seat across from her. "Traffic was lighter than I expected. . ."

"No need to apologize," she said. "I'm just glad I wasn't totally wrong about you."

Solon's brow furrowed.

"I was hoping you were the kind of man who'd drop everything for his son. But I must confess, I was beginning to wonder." Sadie closed the file she'd been working on, dropped her pen into the pencil cup on the edge of her desk. Clearing a space in front of her, she walked her fingers down the stack to her left, and slid a folder from it. "Frankly, what I heard yesterday surprised me a great deal. I didn't have a chance to give it much thought yesterday, or I would have scheduled this appointment when I saw you yesterday." Her voice was cool. "However, I've gone over the tape of my conference with Jesse several times since then." She opened the folder.

Jesse's file, Solon knew. He replanted his feet and squared his shoulders, waiting for her to break the bad news. He'd thought about it all the way over here: Had the boy cut a class? Skipped school altogether? Threatened another student. . . ?

"Jesse thinks you don't love him," she announced, breaking his concentration.

He'd die for that boy! What was she talking about?

With her usual straightforward attitude, Sadie synopsized her meeting with Jesse on the day before. "His resentment is rooted in the assumption that, because he never saw you grieve, you don't miss your wife."

"That's ridiculous," Solon complained, scowling. "Everything I've done, I've done for Jesse!"

"Somehow," Sadie said quietly, "Jesse doesn't see it that way. He says he wishes *you* were dead."

"He'd never say such a thing. . ."

Her face said what words needn't: "I thought you might say that." She put a tape in the recorder on her desk and depressed the play button:

"I wish he was dead," came Jesse's voice. "Then I could do whatever I want without him sticking his nose in my business all the time, pretending it's 'cause he cares." The hiss and crackle of the tape indicated Jesse's pause, and then, "He didn't care about Mama when she died, and I won't care when he bites it."

Sadie switched off the tape recorder, sat back, and looked at the father.

He'd expected to hear that Jesse had broken some school rule. That he hadn't been doing his homework. That he'd had an altercation with a fellow student. Hearing this—that his son didn't believe he was loved—rocked Solon to his very soul. He'd worked like a dog, building his business. Why? To create a legacy for his only child! As much as humanly possible, he'd moved heaven and earth to be home every minute he could spare, to be there, in case Jesse needed him . . .for assistance with homework, to discuss his school day, to shoot a few hoops.

He'd been strong all through Coral's illness. Had held it

together, even after the deadly diagnosis. And when they lost her, he'd kept his grief a dark, private secret, believing it was the best way to protect his only child from feeling that same pain.

So Solon hadn't come apart, not in those first scathing interviews with school guidance counselors, when Jesse first began exhibiting signs of distress. He hadn't shared his own feelings with anyone; even later when the board of education recommended that both he and Jesse meet with a psychologist and then a social worker, he had created a strong facade to show the counselors. Neither Art Johnson nor Joey Mulhearne knew how deeply Coral's death had wounded him; why would he share his grief with these strangers?

The experts' conclusions were amazingly parallel: Jesse, they had determined, had not come to terms with his mother's death; his acting out was a manifestation of unspoken and misplaced anger at Coral for leaving him. Not one of those professionals had dared tell Solon that his way of handling the situation was the real reason for Jesse's behavior!

So unnerved and hurt was he by the news, that Solon's thoughts became his words: "But the boy never came to me for help. Didn't come to talk, either. Did I notice? Sure I noticed! But what could I do? I didn't want to force him to talk about his mama if it hurt him. Didn't want him to see how much her dying hurt me.

"I figured sooner or later, he'd be ready to talk; figured he'd be ready *sooner* if I held it together, if I was strong. My daddy taught me that actions speak louder than words, so I aimed to show him, by the way I conducted my day-to-day life, that life goes on."

Solon scrubbed both hands over his haggard face. "Every day that went by, I could see him growing farther and farther away. I'd reach out, and he'd pull away. I'd ask him what was wrong, and he'd say 'nothing.' I'd ask him how he was, and he'd say 'fine.'

"When Coral was alive, Jesse and me were so *close*.

Hugging, kissing, roughhousing. . ."

The broad shoulders slumped. His chin was nearly touching the knot of his tie when he said, "There we were, father and son, living under the same roof. . .*strangers*."

He sat quietly for a long time, simply shaking his head. When he looked up at Sadie, there were tears in his eyes. "I'm sorry," he said, his voice a gravelly whisper. "I never meant. . ."

She knew the reason for his sudden silence: Solon was mustering the strength to control his emotions. This was not a man accustomed to giving in to whims or moods.

He took a cleansing breath, sat up straighter. "I never meant to. . .This is about *Jesse*, not me. . ."

If there hadn't been a desk between them, she'd likely have wrapped him in a fierce hug and told him everything *was* all right, that everything would be all right. Instead, Sadie acknowledged a personal sin: She'd called him here to boast that her adept counseling skills had unearthed the major cause of Jesse's problems. Pride that she—with barely more than four years in the profession—had not only the talent, but the smarts to see what so many of her more experienced peers had not—that pride had overshadowed everything else.

Her mind raced back to the telephone call to Solon. Get your sorry self down here, and quick, her pompous voice and attitude might as well have said, so I can tell you how you've messed up your kid's life! She remembered thinking that the sharp-dressing, fast-talking businessman who had fathered this lonely boy was going to get a piece of her mind! He always seemed so well put-together, from the sharply creased trousers to the way he walked into a room. Well, he'd be told, she'd decided, in no uncertain terms, that neither his snappy wardrobe nor his successful company were as important as his son's future!

Guilt hammered inside her, for she'd committed one of the most unattractive of human sins. She had judged this man guilty by outward appearances alone, when her Christian upbringing, her career, her *life* should have made clear she should reserve her opinions until all the evidence was in. *And even then*, she further chided herself, *it's the good Lord Who does the judging, not you!*

If she hadn't been so all-fired *wrong* about Solon, Sadie might have been able to salvage some of her self-respect. But there he sat, damp-eyed and disheartened, further proving the arrogance of her quick diagnosis.

She sat up straighter and folded her hands on the desktop. *You'll pray for forgiveness from the Almighty later*, she told herself. *For now, you'll do the right thing. . .*

Taking a deep breath, Sadie plunged in. "Mr. Turner, please forgive the audacity of my vanity. I've been in this line of work long enough to know better. . ."

Beneath the furrowed brows, his dark, damp eyes sparkled.

"I made the mistake of presuming to know your mind. . . and your heart. I should have known from the many talks we've had about Jesse that he has always been first on your list of priorities." Cheeks flaming with humiliation, she lifted her chin slightly. "I can assure you that from here on out, I'll conduct myself with careful professionalism." She raised one brow to add, "There is absolutely no room for assumptions when a child's future is at stake."

Despite everything, Solon smiled slightly. "Don't be so hard on yourself, Miss Burke. You were only acting in Jesse's best interests." The smile grew a bit when he added, "I can hardly hold that against you."

❧

An hour or so after Solon had left, Jesse came bursting into Sadie's office. "You got to erase that tape, Miss Burke. I didn't mean any of that stuff I said yesterday." He sat in the chair where his father had just sat a short time ago, and held his head in his hands. "I was just mad, is all. I didn't mean it." His misty eyes met hers. "I didn't mean what I said. . ."

"But Jesse, you said. . ."

"It ain't what you *say*," he told her, his voice deep and

meaningful, "it's what you *do*." He paused. "I'd hate for my dad to ever hear any of that. . ."

Her heart thundered with guilt and shame as she considered the wisdom of this mere boy's words. Sadie lifted the lid to the recorder and removed the cassette, then pulled a length of tape from the case. "There," she said. "It's as good as forgotten."

Jesse wiped his eyes and stood. "Thanks, Miss Burke," he said from the door. "I'll see you tomorrow?"

"Yes, Jesse," she said quietly, forcing a smile. "Same time. . . And, Jesse? Maybe you could try letting your dad know— with both your words and your actions—that you still care about him."

Guilt could hardly describe what she felt. It would take a long, long time to make all this up to Solon. Where to start? She picked up the phone. First, she needed to let him know what his son had just said.

❧

For the third Easter in a row, the family would gather around the long mahogany table in the dining room of the house Sadie had bought after her first year at work. The quaint end-of-row house in Baltimore City's historic Fells Point had needed plenty of work before she and her mother could move in, but even that had been a blessing in disguise. The work had distracted her mother from the death of her beloved second husband and had kept Sadie's mind off her horrendous almost-wedding day.

Faith Peters stopped peeling potatoes long enough to ask "When was the last time you basted that turkey, Sadie?"

"Ten minutes ago, Mama." Sadie spooned the last of the fudge icing onto the devil's food cake she'd baked earlier that morning. "How soon do you think we ought to put the ham in?"

Faith lifted one brow. "What time did you tell everybody we'd eat?"

"Three o'clock, as usual."

"Then we'll put in the ham an hour before that. . .it just

needs warming up. . ."

Sadie knew of no family but hers that served both turkey and ham on Easter Sunday. But then, Sadie knew very few families like her own.

Hannah, Carleen, and Cal Junior would arrive an hour earlier than the rest, as in years past. But this year, Floyd Barnes would be in tow. . .Sadie shook her head and grinned. When Calvin had left for places unknown, her sister had vowed never to so much as speak to a man again. And then, like the miracle it was, just one date with Floyd, following on the heels of the divorce she'd never asked for, and Hannah was talking about a vow of an entirely different kind. . .

She was so *happy* for Hannah! The poor woman had scrimped and saved, working harder than anyone else at the KinderKare studio she'd managed all these years. A natural-born teacher, Hannah had the three- and four-year-olds in her care reading and writing before they left her for public school's version of kindergarten. "The job doesn't pay much," her sister often said, "but some rewards simply aren't green!"

Mama had also invited Gladys and Homer, the elderly couple who lived next door. "Their kids all live so far away," Faith had said. "I can't stand to think of them over there in that big house all by themselves, eating canned tuna and drinking tap water on such a special day!"

She'd invited her deceased husband's sister, too. "I'm the only family she has, now that James is gone."

Sadie liked old Sissy Peters nearly as much as she'd liked James. He might have technically been a stepfather, but Sadie couldn't have loved her mother's second husband more. He'd been gone nearly two years now, and she missed him still.

Pastor Higgins, also newly widowed, would almost round out the dozen people who would share the Easter meal. Each had insisted on preparing something to share with the others. Sissy would bring baked beans, Gladys her home-baked biscuits, Hannah her world-famous potato salad. . .

When she'd suggested that Jesse and Solon accompany

them to services, Solon had begged off, saying he hadn't been to church in years. But his son had seemed genuinely interested in meeting her family, and so on impulse Sadie had invited both of them to join her family for Easter dinner. She couldn't very well have invited the son and not the father, now could she? She'd been amazed at how quickly he'd said yes when she'd posed the question on the phone earlier. . .

"What's that silly grin all about?" her mother asked.

Sadie wriggled her shoulders, hoping the action would shake an explanation from her mind. "I can't decide whether to use the white napkins or the blue ones," she said, a finger to her lips.

Faith eyed her warily. "Oh, that look on your face couldn't have anything to do with the handsome young man you've invited to dinner, now could it?"

Hannah had visited Sadie's office during the past week and had met Solon Turner. From that moment on, when any aspect of Sadie's work came up, her sister found a way to bring Jesse's father into the conversation. Though her mother had never met the man face to face, Sadie was certain Faith would be able to pick him out of a crowd, thanks to the detailed picture Hannah had drawn.

Sadie glanced at the clock. She'd always been a talented and inventive cook, and though a surgeon could perform operations in her kitchen *after* she'd cleaned up a meal, she'd never been the tidiest chef. And so she'd changed into a baggy sweatsuit after Easter Sunday services. Now she faced a dilemma: Slip back into the classy suit she'd worn to church, or something more. . .

"I think you ought to wear your pink dress," her mother was saying. "Makes you look so young and beautiful." Faith rolled her eyes. "That poor man likely thinks you play tennis in a business suit. Might be just the nudge he needs, to see you in something soft and feminine."

"Mama!" Sadie shook her finger at her mother. "My relationship with Mr. Turner is strictly—"

"Might not be 'strictly business,'" Faith interrupted her daughter, "if you'd. . ."

Sadie had never spoken a disrespectful word to her mother in all her life, and she didn't intend to start now. Still. . .the woman could sometimes be exasperating, the way she was forever trying to fix her up with eligible young men. . . "Not that there's much point in my telling you—since Hannah has given you everything, including his shoe size—but as you'll see, Mr. Turner isn't interested in anything but a professional relationship." In response to her mother's knowing grin, Sadie quickly added "Either" to her sentence.

Faith fanned her hands beside her cheeks. "No need to get all hot under the collar, girl. If you say it's all business, then it's all business."

Sadie eyed her warily as she passed her on her way to the stairs. "I'm going to get cleaned up now."

"All right, honey," Faith said. And the minute she believed her daughter out of earshot, added a quiet, "But you *want* to mix business with pleasure, if you ask me!"

"I heard that, Mama," Sadie whispered as she ran up the steps, "but since there's no point arguing with you, I won't."

Closing the door to her room, she glanced at the latest work of art on her easel. She'd started it several weeks earlier, with no sketch, no plan, no idea what it might be when complete. Sadie had decided to allow her whimsical, artistic side to dictate what she'd paint.

Telling herself she'd just been in a heavy mood because of all the depressing cases she'd been handling, Sadie had allowed herself to work in mostly black, gray, and brown tones. Soon, the image took human shape: masculine, broad chinned, dark. It hadn't looked familiar to her before this; why hadn't she noticed the similarities till now?

Quickly, before her mother (or heaven forbid, Hannah!) could see the likeness, Sadie draped the canvas with a discarded pillowcase.

You *want* to mix business with pleasure, if you ask me, her mother had said moments earlier. Covering the portrait couldn't hide the truth that lived in her subconscious: Her mother was right!

≈

She'd told him to dress casually, though she wondered if he knew the meaning of the word. Sadie had never seen him in anything but a crisply pressed business suit. When he strode down the walk, balancing a gingham-covered plate on his right palm, Sadie couldn't help but smile.

In place of the sleek, polished loafers he usually wore, a pair of high-topped Reeboks covered his feet. Blue jeans encased his muscular legs, and a soft blue mock turtleneck sweater clung to his broad chest.

"Hi," Solon said, grinning as she opened the front door wider. "I really like your neighborhood, even if parking is a pain in the neck."

She stepped aside as he entered the foyer. "It's even worse in the evening, and on weekends. . ." She pressed a hand to her chest. "But don't get me started on politics," she said, closing the door.

Jesse followed his father into the foyer, and Sadie nonchalantly slipped an arm over Jesse's shoulders. "My, but don't you both look handsome today!" Leaning closer, she whispered into the boy's ear, "Good thing, too, 'cause my mama's the old-fashioned type; she doesn't take to folks coming to the dinner table in droopy drawers."

She hadn't expected the boy to smile, let alone chuckle at her comment, and she had to ask herself if she'd ever heard him laugh before.

Laughing with them, Solon extended the hand that held the napkin-covered plate. "Would you like me to put these in the kitchen?"

"*These?*" she repeated, narrowing one eye. To Jesse, she said, "'These' is plural; so there's a mess of something under that napkin." Sadie sniffed the air. "Chocolate. . .hm-m-m. . ." Laying a finger against her cheek, she added, "Now the question is, which of Jesse's favorites is it: brownies or chocolate chip cookies?"

The boy gave her a startled look. "How'd you know. . . ?"

Sadie gave him an affectionate sideways hug. "You don't think all your father and I talk about are your *grades*, do you? I believe you'd be surprised at all the mushy things I've learned about you!"

He shot a glance in his father's direction, and as they had when he'd asked her to erase the tape, Jesse's eyes gleamed with love and admiration. His father beamed proudly back at his son.

Something private and personal had happened there, right before Sadie's eyes. What exactly, she didn't know, but she had a feeling that it was one step of many in the right direction.

"And what do we have here?" Faith clapped her hands together as she entered the foyer. "I'm Sadie's mama," she said, grabbing the plate from Solon. Peeking under the napkin, she placed her free hand over her heart. "If that don't beat all, my very favorite dessert in the entire world! How'd you know, Mr. Turner? Did my girl tell you?"

Chuckling, he released her hand. "Please, call me Solon. And yes, your daughter did tell me that your favorite dessert is. . ."

"Double fudge brownies!" Faith gushed. Suddenly, her smile faded slightly. The gleam in her eye shone brighter than ever when she added, "It's a real shame that deep-dish apple pie you baked is gonna go to waste, honey. Who wants ordinary dessert when you can have *brownies*?"

Sadie, giggling softly, relieved her mother of the plate. "I'll just put these in the kitchen," she said. "What can I get you gentlemen to drink. Iced tea? Lemonade? Soda?"

"I'll take a. . ."

"Pepsi," Sadie finished for Jesse.

His grin told her Jesse was pleased that she knew this seemingly insignificant fact about him. "And you, Solon?

What would you like?"

I'd like you, he thought, "Pepsi will be fine, as long as you're pouring one for Jesse. . ."

He watched her walk down the short hall and out of sight, thinking as she did that Sadie Burke was quite possibly the prettiest little thing he'd ever seen. She moved with the grace of a gazelle, each step feminine and sure and alluring. He'd never seen her in a real dress before. The pale pink material of her bodice skimmed her waist, accenting her delicate frame, and ended in a dainty flounce just above her knees. She wore white flats on her tiny feet, and she'd pinned her curly hair back from her face with two white combs. He'd thought she was pretty under the harsh white florescent lights in her office, dressed in her severe, no-nonsense suits, but here in the warm light of her sunny foyer, as she was wearing something soft and feminine, her complexion looked even more like soft caramel than ever. He thought she'd never looked lovelier.

"Well, come here and give me a hello hug, son," Faith said, interrupting Solon's thoughts. Smiling, he watched the little woman pull his son into a welcoming embrace. His smile broadened a bit at Jesse's happy reaction to the affectionate attention. She turned his boy loose and faced Solon. Waving her hands, she invited him to step forward. "You, too," she ordered. "Nobody comes into my home without getting a proper welcome." He had to bend down to let her get a grip, but he found once she did that she was surprisingly strong for a woman of her size and age. He put Faith at fifty-five or sixty years of age, and wondered what Sadie would be like when she. . .

The doorbell chimed, forcing Faith to unhand him. "Get on into the parlor and make yourselves comfortable," she instructed, pointing the way as she threw open the door. "What are you doing ringing the bell like some ordinary company?" she demanded, drawing her grandchildren into her arms. "Hannah, after you put your potato salad in the fridge, bring each of my sweet babies one of those brownies this nice man brought."

She hadn't yet closed the door behind them when a thick-middled man stepped onto the porch. "How kind of you to invite me to dinner, Mrs. Peters."

Facing the man on the porch, her grandmotherly de-meanor vanished. Pressing a dainty hand to her well-coiffed hair, she smiled. "And how kind of you to agree to say the blessing for us. Please, won't you come in and join us in the parlor?"

"Good to see you again so soon, Hannah, Carleen, Calvin," Pastor Higgins said.

Before Hannah had a chance to respond, Faith said, "While you're in the kitchen, pour the good pastor a tall glass of cold lemonade, won't you?"

The friendly chit-chat continued until Sadie announced that dinner was served. Soon, all the guests gathered around the table in the bright dining room. Pastor Higgins, whom Faith forced to sit at the head of the table, stood and summoned silence. And then the man who needed no microphone to preach his sermons said in a hushed, serene voice, "Will you all join me in a prayer?"

Immediately, the chatter ceased. Every head bowed, and all hands were folded as he continued, "Lord God in heaven, we thank You for the good health that enables us to be here, cele-brating Your Resurrection this day. We thank You, yes, Lord, for this bountiful feast and the talented women who prepared it. Thank You, Lord, for surrounding us with good friends and companions. Bless these folks, Lord, and this food we're about to eat. We ask all these things in Your holy name."

And those gathered joined him in saying, "Amen."

The pastor clasped his hands together and grinned. "Now, then," he said, sitting, "who's going to pass the ham?"

The conversation was light and cheerful as bowls of steaming vegetables, platters of meat, and baskets of biscuits were passed up and down the table. Solon watched with amazement as his son, who sat between Hannah's children, talked as though he'd known Cal Junior and Carleen for years. He'd rejected invitations like this one many times, afraid that being surrounded by family warmth would only remind Jesse that he'd lost his mother. Seeing the boy now—animated, smiling, laughing at Cal Junior's antics— Solon realized that hiding from the past had not protected Jesse from painful memories. Rather, evading their history had caused a great deal of damage. If he had still been on a first-name basis with God, Solon would have asked His forgiveness for all the mistakes he'd made with Jesse; might have prayed for a way to make it all up to his son. As it was, he'd have to be content with the hope that Sadie's influence—and his own resolve to be more open and honest about his feelings—would help turn the boy around.

After dinner, Sadie insisted upon washing up the dishes alone. After shooing the children into the backyard, she ushered Pastor Harris, Hannah, Floyd and Faith, and her neighbors into the parlor. While the others enjoyed coffee and quiet conversation, Solon followed Sadie back into the kitchen. She positioned herself at the sink, looking up often through the kitchen window to watch the kids' spirited game of touch football.

"He seems so happy," she observed, rinsing a plate.

"You've made a huge difference in his life, Sadie. You know I didn't think this dinner was a good idea at first—but I'm glad I let you talk me into it."

She shrugged one shoulder and rinsed another plate. "Just doin' my job."

His heart swelled with an emotion he'd thought long dead . . .three years dead to be exact. Solon reached into the sudsy water and wrapped his hand around her wrist.

"Solon," she said, giggling, "your sleeve is getting wet. And your watch is covered with suds. . ."

Wet? Sudsy? Solon didn't notice. . .didn't care what condition his shirt or his timepiece were in. "Art Johnson was right."

She met his eyes then. "About what?"

"You're a wonderful woman." *And if you don't get to know her better*, he recalled Johnson's warning, *you're a fool*. "I'd like. . .I'd like to get to know you better."

Her big eyes widened further in response to his simple statement. She blinked several times, ran her tongue over her lips, as if considering the meaning behind his words.

Solon smiled. "I'd consider it an honor if you'd agree to have dinner with me sometime. I've. . .I've been out of commission for a while. . . I'll let you choose the restaurant." He was still holding her wrist when he added, "What's your favorite, Italian? Chinese? Mexican?"

"Solon," she began, "I. . .I don't know what to say."

He took a step closer, linked his fingers with hers in the warm, bubbly water. "Say yes."

If she keeps looking at you that way, Solon told himself, *you're not going to have any choice but to kiss her*. Coral's sweet face hovered in his mind, and yet he smiled. It was as if his dear wife, knowing her husband would never step out on his own and find a woman, had stood him here herself, in Sadie's tidy white kitchen. He remembered all too clearly their last conversation, when Coral had forced him to promise he'd not turn away when love came knocking. Remembered, too, the piece of advice Art Johnson had given him, mere weeks ago: She wasn't the kind of woman who would have wanted you to climb into the coffin with her, Solon. She had a heart as big as Texas. If she knew what you were doing to yourself, she'd scold you good and sound.

He hadn't thought it possible to love that way again, so Solon hadn't bothered to search for a woman to share his life. Sure, he'd endured the blind dates set up by well-meaning friends. But not one of the ladies, no matter how lovely, could compare to his sweet Coral.

But that was before he'd met Sadie. And right from the moment he walked into her organized little office—though he'd denied it and fought it with everything in him—he'd felt a tug at his heartstrings.

There was no point denying it anymore. He was crazy about this little woman, not only because of the small improvements he'd begun to see in Jesse's behavior, but also because of the improvements he'd begun to see in his own behavior.

If he took another step closer, he'd be pressed against her right side. *And if you keep looking at me that way*, he repeated mentally. . .

The sunlight, streaming in through the window above the sink, kissed her bronzed cheek and danced in her eyes like a hundred little sparklers. He hadn't noticed before that her gold-red eyes were flecked with brown, and green, and black. Hadn't noticed before just how long and lush her lashes were. . .

"Solon," she whispered, "I. . ."

"Shhh," he whispered back.

And then he closed his eyes, and he kissed her.

six

Baltimore's traditional sultry breezes caressed Sadie's face and hair as she plucked dying flowers from the plants. The pastel buds and blossoms of Easter had given way to the bright splashes of summer flowers and leafy trees. She was proud of her colorful, weed-free beds. Proud of the spring onions, radishes, and lettuce that grew in the vegetable garden, too. She liked to think of herself as the mother of these plants, and gave them all the maternal care they required. Believing they'd likely be the only "children" she'd ever have, Sadie showered them with attention.

Inside, a virtual jungle bloomed. Houseplants of every variety hung from poles and wall racks, stood on plant stands, end tables, and floors. Daily, she inspected them for signs of mold, fungus, whiteflies. Weekly, she watered and fertilized and rid the main stems of withering leaves and shoots.

She was pruning her prized hibiscus when that first kiss resonated in her mind. He'd given her many more to match it since that sunny Easter Sunday, but it was *that* one. . .that sweet and daring one. . .that Sadie would remember all the days of her life.

He'd reminded her of a small child, moving closer, one hesitant step at a time, an expectant, hopeful look gleaming in his dark eyes. She'd known for some time before the kiss that what she felt for Solon went far beyond professional bounds, but in the first, fleeting, fantastic moments of that kiss, Sadie realized, happily, that he'd been feeling something more for her, too.

There was no telling how long it might have lasted, or if it might have inspired a second. . .a third. . .if her sister hadn't barged into the room in typical Hurricane Hannah way.

"Goodness gracious sakes alive," she'd said, pouting, hands on her hips. "Mama said you had your heads together in here over the 'Jesse thing,' but this gives a whole new meaning to the cliché!"

Even after the brusk interruption, he'd seemed reluctant to end the kiss, to step away, to release her hand which was still submerged in the dishpan. Solon had taken a deep breath and let it out slowly. Had shaken his head and said, never taking his eyes from Sadie's, "Hannah, I appreciate the sense of humor required to make such a comment, but you could never be a comedienne. . .your sense of timing is horrible."

Laughing, Hannah had dismissed herself, saying over her shoulder as she went, "Fine, then! See if I offer to help you with the dishes again!" And though he'd stayed near to Sadie's side long after Hannah was gone, he hadn't attempted to begin again what her sister had ended.

There were had been other kisses in Sadie's memory book, but not one had ever before started her heart to beating like a parade drum. Standing in the circle of a young man's arms had never made her feel protected and warm and wanted, all at the same time. And she'd never seen in another's eyes a look that blended admiration, respect, and yearning.

She'd prayed long and hard about her feelings for Solon: Is *this* the man You intend me to spend the rest of my life with? Am I the woman You believe best for Solon and Jesse? But so far, the good Lord had decided not to write His answer across the sky, hadn't trumpeted a reply by way of inspirational song, hadn't sent a message via the pages of her Bible. Sadie's heart wanted to believe that her ever-increasing love for Solon might be the Almighty's response, and her mind hoped the lengthening list of his finer qualities was a sign from above. But letting her dreams and wishes drive her interpretation of God's will had cost her in the past. Sadie was not willing to pay such a hefty price again, and she was determined to wait and see what the Lord had in mind for her, for Solon, for Jesse.

Solon, she believed, had been grappling with the same issues. He hadn't said it in so many words, but Sadie was beginning to believe that maybe he loved her, too. She sensed this for many reasons, among them the way he'd changed since that first kiss in her kitchen. He smiled often now, and the light of his joy seemed to begin in his heart and emanate all the way up to his dark smoldering eyes. He went with her to church now, and he seemed to have opened his wounded heart to the good Lord's healing love. And though she had been surprised, at first, to discover he had such a good sense of humor, she hadn't taken long to delight in his jokes.

The most noticeable change was in the way he treated— and reacted to—his son. Solon had told her about the coveted builders' award he hoped to be nominated to receive. Had told her, too, that if he didn't keep his finger on the pulse of the industry, the prize was as good as gone.

Yet he worked fewer hours. Spent more and more time at Thornton, repairing this and that. Set aside more and more time to be with Jesse, playing basketball, jogging, plain talking.

And every chance he got, Solon made time for *her*.

Sadie had quizzed him about this just last week. "What chance do you think you have of winning the plaque if you keep cancelling meetings to take me to dinner and a movie?"

Solon had shrugged, assuming a "who cares?" expression, and said, "If I win, I win. If I don't, I'm still the luckiest man in the state of Maryland."

Sadie didn't know how long she'd been kneeling there among the daisies and the chrysanthemums, remembering. . . Sighing, she pulled back the sleeve of her gardening glove to peek at her wristwatch and read a quarter after three. Solon would arrive in less than two hours, to treat her to "something really special." As if all their dates hadn't been special!

But he'd insisted that since tomorrow she'd turn twenty-eight, they must celebrate like they'd never celebrated before. "Wear comfortable shoes and blue jeans," he'd instructed that morning on the phone, "and tie all that gorgeous hair of yours into a ponytail, and. . ."

"Spencer Christian is predicting rain," she'd warned.

"That weatherman's all wet; ain't nobody gonna rain on our parade!" Solon insisted. "This is gonna be a day you won't soon forget!"

Standing, Sadie dusted mulch from the knees of her khakis and slipped her gloves and pruning shears into the basket of gardening tools. After locking the tiny potting shed she'd built single-handedly last summer, she headed for the house to shower and change for her birthday surprise.

Jesse and Solon arrived exactly five minutes to five, looking more like brothers than father and son. Each wore high-topped sneakers and jeans. "Orioles," said Jesse's white cotton T-shirt. "The Baltimore Ravens," boasted Solon's.

Sadie had worn white jeans, white sneakers, and a black-and-white striped long-sleeved T-shirt. A black scrunchie held her thick hair in a high ponytail. "Mm-m-m, mm-m-m, *mm-m-m* girl, I'm tempted to say you're as pretty as a picture, 'cept I've never seen a picture pretty as you," Solon said as she slid into the Explorer's passenger seat.

For some strange reason, the painting that had surprisingly turned out to be Solon flashed in her mind. What would he say if he knew she'd committed him to canvas? she wondered, grinning.

"I packed us a picnic supper," Jesse announced as Solon started the motor. "Fried chicken, potato chips, Oreos, and Pepsi." Snickering, he added, "Good thing you guys aren't a few years older; we learned in health class that this is the kind of meal that clogs old people's arteries."

Sadie's giggle filled the Ford's interior. "If we were old people," she asked, turning in her seat to face him, "what kind of picnic would you have packed?"

He squinted and pursed his lips as he considered the alternatives. "I guess I'd just buy a dozen or so jars of baby food." Grinning, he added, "That way, if you two forgot to put in your false teeth, you could still eat a nutritious, well-balanced meal."

"The Lord works in mysterious ways," Solon observed.

Sadie and Jesse looked at him, waiting for the explanation they knew would follow.

"He advises, by way of the Bible, children to care for their parents when they get old and feeble. I can rest easy knowing my boy is gonna follow the rules."

Jesse had come a long way in a short time. Suddenly, his one semester at Thornton seemed to have been enough to straighten him out. When this blistering Baltimore summer ended, he'd re-enroll as one of Art Johnson's sophomores. And Sadie believed the principal would have no more trouble with Jesse Turner!

She knew their one-on-one counseling sessions had contributed to Jesse's newfound positive attitude. But there was no escaping the real reason for his turn-around: He knew now that his father loved him.

Doing and saying the things that showed his son how he felt had not been an easy feat for a man who'd spent his life keeping his emotions to himself. But Solon, once he'd realized that hiding his feelings had hurt, rather than helped his son, made Jesse his first priority.

"When we gonna tell her where we're going, Dad?"

"When we get there she'll know where she is."

Sadie shook her head and feigned exasperation. "I think it's mean and cruel, keeping me in the dark this way."

Solon held his hands in a gesture of surrender. "Hey, all this suspense and subterfuge wasn't my idea." Using his thumb to point over his shoulder, he added, "Register your complaints with James Bond back there."

Sadie turned as far as the seat belt would allow. "Jesse. . . all this secrecy was *your* idea?" She pouted prettily. "And I thought you *liked* me!"

Every tooth in his head showed when he grinned back at

her. "I *do* like you. That's why I wanted to be sure your birthday was. . ."

"Special," they both said together.

"Well, then," Sadie said, facing front again, "I guess I'm just going to have to exercise a bit more patience." Not a minute went by before she asked, "When will we get there?"

Solon adjusted the radio dial and tuned in a soft rock station. The song that had been playing when he depressed the channel selector had barely ended when she said again, "Are we there yet?"

"Not yet. . ."

She sang along with the next two songs, then said, "How much longer?"

Jesse laughed. "Who's she remind you of, Dad?"

Solon laughed, too. "She reminds me of a certain persistent little boy, that's who," he said, wheeling the Explorer onto an off-ramp. At the stop sign, he turned right.

Soon road signs told Sadie what Solon and Jesse would not: They were on their way to Hershey Park, Pennsylvania's most famous amusement park. She hadn't ridden a roller coaster, a Ferris wheel, or a merry-go-round since. . .well, Sadie honestly couldn't remember the last time she'd screamed like a girl as the Tilt-o-Whirl and the Octopus whipped her into a dizzy frenzy.

The three of them rode nearly every ride, Sadie sandwiched between Solon and Jesse, stopping only to head for the car at supper time, where they spent no more than twenty minutes munching the goodies Jesse had jammed into the big brown wicker picnic basket. Stars were twinkling above them as they headed home, pleasantly exhausted from laughing and squealing. Jesse held tight to the goldfish he'd won in the ping-pong ball-toss game. Solon gripped a gigantic red bear under his arm. . .his prize for slinging a ring over a pencil-thin post. Sadie wore her trophy home: A baggy white T-shirt that read "I Survived the Sooper-Dooper Looper."

She'd treasure it until the letters faded, and she told Solon and Jesse, "That's likely how long I'll be hoarse from all the screaming!"

When they parked in Sadie's black-topped driveway, the porch light told them Faith had retired for the night. "Would you two care for a midnight snack?"

"Would I?" Jesse responded. "I'm starving!"

Solon pretended to grimace. "Haven't fed him in. . ." he checked his watch. ". . .in nearly an hour."

The Turner men sat at her kitchen table, sipping home-squeezed lemonade, as Sadie whipped up Dagwood-style sandwiches. She chattered nonstop as she piled ham, cheese, lettuce, and tomatoes on big ovals of rye bread. "I *should* have let you buy me that cotton candy," she said, "because now my mouth is watering for one!"

Sadie nibbled at her sandwich as they devoured theirs, marveling at how much like his father Jesse had become. Like any boy of fourteen going on fifteen, he had a few rough edges. Take the way he thought belching in public was funny, rather than rude, for example. And the way he liked to turn every activity into a good-natured competition, from who got into the car first to who could use the rest rooms fastest. Even this, eating sandwiches, became a playful contest. He seemed intent upon being first, fastest, best, and something told her he'd inherited his drive to be at the head of the line from his father.

Solon had only finished half of his sandwich when Jesse stretched and yawned. "Mind if I see what's on TV?"

"Not at all," Sadie said. "The remote is. . ."

". . .on top of the television," he finished for her as he left the room.

The sounds of his rapid-fire channel surfing filtered into the kitchen as Solon reached across the table and took Sadie's hand. "Did I tell you how gorgeous you look tonight?"

"Only a hundred times or so," she said, giggling.

"So, did you enjoy your birthday?"

"I can't remember a better one."

He let go of her hand, slid his own into his pants pocket. "I wanted to give you this while we were alone," he said, withdrawing a small velvet box. "I would have wrapped it, but then you'd have known how *un*artistic I am."

Smiling, Sadie said, "Men aren't supposed to be good at things like wrapping packages. That's why God gave 'em women!"

The bright smile in his eyes took on a warmer, gentler light. "I don't know why He chose to put you in my life, Sadie," he said, his voice a near whisper, "but I thank Him every chance I get. Was a time not too long ago," his voice wavered, "that the Almighty and I weren't even on speaking terms. But that's all changed now. Thanks to you."

She didn't know how to react to that, and hoped he couldn't hear the hammering of her heart. Smiling softly, she said, "I've sent a grateful prayer heavenward a time or two, myself."

He didn't seem at all surprised to hear this, and Sadie was glad. Neither of them had spoken aloud of their feelings, but plenty of others had commented on what *they'd* seen. . .

He slid the box nearer her hand. "Go on. Open it."

Sadie hesitated for an instant, as much because she didn't want to move her hand from beneath his as for any other reason. It was the size and shape of Evan's engagement ring's box. She loved this man, loved his son, too, but she was suddenly worried that perhaps it was too soon for a declaration of this depth. . .

"Are you *trying* to drive me crazy?" he asked, interrupting her self-inquisition. "Ever since I bought the gift, I've been dying to know how you'd like it."

She took a deep breath, then wrapped her hand around the fuzzy little container. The lid creaked slightly as she opened it. Inside, from a pillowy bed of shining white satin, two diamond studs winked up at her.

"Solon," she sighed, "they're. . .they're *beautiful*."

"The moment I saw them, I thought of you. . .tiny and genuine and shiny as the North Star." He paused, then added,

"If they're not big enough, I can take them back. . ."

"Take them back! But Solon, they're *perfect*!" And to prove it, she immediately attempted to remove the dangling hoops she'd worn to Hershey Park. Unfortunately, she found that her hands were trembling too hard to accomplish the task.

"Here," he said, smiling as he walked around to her side of the table, "let me help you." He turned her chair around so that she faced him directly, and got onto one knee. Then, ever so gently and wearing an expression of intense concentration, he unhooked the gold earrings and laid them on the table. "There," he said, "now, would you like me to put the studs in, or would you prefer to do that yourself?"

With her seated in the chair, and Solon kneeling at her feet, they were eye to eye. . .and nearly nose to nose as well. "I'd like you to do it, if you don't mind," she whispered.

She noticed that his hands were shaking too as he separated the tiny backings from the posts. Each earring seemed to disappear in his thick fingers, and yet he managed to coax the jewels into her earlobes with amazing dexterity for a man of his size.

"Let me have a look at you," he said when he'd finished. Leaning back slightly, Solon cradled her face in both hands, tilted her head left, then right, to catch the light that beamed from the Tiffany fixture over her table. "They glitter and gleam," he said, staring deep into her eyes, "but they can't begin to compare to the fire in your eyes."

Dear Lord in heaven, Sadie prayed, *I love him as I've never loved a man before. Just look at the way he looks at me. . .as though I, personally, hung the moon!* Smiling, she blinked back tears of joy. When Evan left her at the altar, she'd decided to dedicate her life to others. Marriage, children, love, none of them seemed to be in the cards for her. And then, smack in the middle of her busy do-for-others life, God sent her Solon! *I don't know what I ever did to deserve a man like this*, she added, *but thank You for sending him to me!*

Sadie was suddenly so overcome with emotion that she had no choice but to throw her arms around his neck and hug him tight. "Did anyone ever tell you what a wonderful, generous, big-hearted man you are?"

His quiet chuckle tickled her ear. Shrugging, he said, "Oh, I hear it a couple times a day, at least."

Solon held her at arm's length and looked from her eyes to her hair, from her cheeks to her lips. "You do look happy, girl. I guess this is what they mean when they say 'smiling from ear to ear.'" Then, "Did anyone ever tell you that you have the face of an angel?"

She lifted one brow. "I told you on the day we met. . .you'd find neither halo nor wings on me."

His lips grazed her cheek as he said, "Without wings and a halo, some angels wouldn't be recognized as angels. But you," he added, pressing a light kiss to each of her eyelids, "don't need the obvious adornments."

He began to list her many positive character traits with such meticulous attention to detail that Sadie instantly understood the mind of the man who had taken a dime-a-dozen shoestring operation to the third largest construction company in the DelMarVa Peninsula. She was honest, he said, hard-working, caring, dedicated. . .But Sadie refused to focus on the flattery. What she *really* wanted him to say was that he loved her. Because if he did, she'd shoot the words right back at him so fast, he'd likely end up sitting on her kitchen floor! It crossed her mind that, if she said the words first, Solon might feel free to return the words to her. . .

But something—Jesse in the next room watching TV, Solon's obvious heartache for Coral that day in her office, fear that she'd just been fooling herself all along—made her bite back the words. She could not trust her own heart. . .hadn't it believed Evan's lies? Couldn't trust her own mind, either, for it had sifted through her fiancé's words, believing those that sounded pretty, rejecting those that rang with warning. She *could* trust God. *He* would not mislead or trick her; *He* would guide her toward the truth. . .if she had the good sense and patience to let Him.

Sadie decided right then and there to put her self-doubt at the foot of the Cross. If this blossoming relationship was what the Lord intended for them, He would make it clear. . . in time. If not, He would give them all the strength to bear up under the pain of separation.

In the meantime, she would revel in Solon's goodness and decency. In the meantime, Sadie would simply enjoy his presence in her life. He was still naming her positive traits when she tilted her head back slightly, closed her eyes, and said in a playful, Greta Garbo imitation, "Shut up and kiss me, you fool."

And when he did, Sadie's heart made a joyful noise.

❧

A few months later, Rasheed and his gang surrounded Jesse, then pressed in close. "You been askin' for this whoopin' since the day I met you," the leader snarled.

If he walked away from this crowd with no broken bones, Jesse would count himself lucky. If he walked away with his life, he'd count himself *blessed*.

He'd heard rumors about Rasheed's control over the Leakin Park neighborhood, and so he'd avoided entering Bloods' territory. He hadn't anticipated the gang coming into *his* world. . .

"You think you better than the rest of us, but you *ain't*."

He had no desire to die on this crisp fall afternoon. He'd asked Carleen to go to the movies with him, and she'd accepted. His grades were better than they'd been since before his mama died, and his relationship with Solon had never been stronger. As if all that wasn't enough to live for, it was beginning to look as if Sadie might just agree to become his stepmother. . .

"You no better than us," Rasheed spat out. "You just a uppity little black boy whose daddy got lucky, is all."

His father's achievements had nothing to do with luck, and

he told Rasheed so. "He was born on Milton Street, and grew up poor, just like you," Jesse said. "His daddy worked hard and died young, and his mama did, too. He could have joined a gang, sold drugs, *used* drugs. . .could have blamed the Man for all his troubles. But he didn't want to end up a loser, like you. He knew right from wrong, and—"

"We didn't come all the way to your fancy neighborhood to hear fairy tales, Jester. We been looking to find you alone, so we could settle up."

Jesse ignored Rasheed's not-so-veiled threat. "There's nothing to settle."

"That's what you think, fool. You could a got my brother, Mohammed, here, killed in that store. You was supposed to *help* him, not *fight* him. He—"

"He was going to kill a man over a couple packages of *cookies*, Rasheed. Way I figure it, I saved him from spending his life at Jessup."

"How the Man gonna know Mohammed be the shooter?" Rasheed growled. "You was gonna rat him out?"

Jesse said through clenched teeth, "I wouldn't have had to say a word. The whole thing was being filmed by a security camera." He glared at the boys who danced to Rasheed's tune. "Don't you case a place before you try to rob it? Didn't you know there was a surveillance device?"

"Listen to him," Rasheed interrupted. "Talkin' like some white boy who watches all them cop shows on TV. 'Case the place,'" he mocked. "'Surveillance device.'" His laughter inspired the others to follow suit. "You might be black on the outside, Jester," he hissed, "but you ain't one of us. You's what we call an Oreo—black where it shows but white on the inside."

This was a challenge that, if met, could very well end his life. But, the way Jesse saw it, he wasn't likely to walk away from this unscathed, anyway. *May as well give them a thing or two to think about before you go down*, he told himself. He said a quick prayer for protection, then said in a bold, brave voice, "I don't want to be one of you. 'The Man' isn't holding us down all by himself, people *like* you are just as much to blame when—"

"Shut *up*, fool!" Rasheed shouted. "You lookin' to get cut, right now?"

Jesse plunged on, seemingly mindless of the possible consequences. "I'm proud of my race," he said, "and there's no denying we've been oppressed. But if men like my father can break through and prove themselves, *others* can do it, too. I want to be someone who makes a difference, like my—"

"You ain't gonna live long enough to make a difference," Rasheed said, pulling a small, dull-black handgun from behind his back. "*This* what make the Man pay attention. *This* what make 'em know we ain't gonna let 'em keep us down."

"Only thing keeping you down, Rasheed, is you," Jesse said. Then, nodding at the gun, he added, "And that. You haven't given them a chance to keep you down; you're doing that, all by yourself, by pretending to be a victim."

Rasheed's eyes glowed like hot coals. He tossed the gun to the ground and leapt onto Jesse, all fists and fire and fury. "I ain't no victim," he bellowed, "but *you* gonna be one when I get done with you!"

When the scuffle began, Jesse gave as good as he got, and when the rest of the Bloods saw this, they stepped forward to assist their leader. "Leave him be," Rasheed ordered. "I want him all to myself."

The gang backed off, and formed a tight circle around the fighters, punching the air and shouting advice to Rasheed. But despite the fact that their warlord was taller, broader, heavier than Jesse, he couldn't seem to land another blow.

What Jesse lacked in size, strength, and street savvy, he made up for with quickness and agility, neatly side-stepping nearly every one of Rasheed's powerful blows. The larger boy, with mounting frustration and rage, and breathing hard, was sweating profusely as Jesse weaved and bobbed and dodged every strike. Rasheed threw a wild left hook with bad intentions, but Jesse nimbly avoided the punch, and caught the lunging Bloods' leader on the jaw with a blow of his own, dropping him to the pavement.

The noise from the circle had dimmed quite a bit by the time a squad car rolled up beside the curb. "What happened to you?" the tall black cop demanded of Rasheed, unsheathing his nightstick as he stepped from the car.

"Nothin'," he said, scrambling to his feet. "Just took a fall, is all."

The cop snickered. "Looks like you took it from a ten-story building."

Rasheed's gang hid their grins and chuckles behind gold-ringed fingers. "Shut up," he sneered, glaring at his retreating army, "or you'll get—"

"We got a complaint from a neighbor," said the cop's Hispanic partner, slapping his own billy club against his palm, "that there was a street fight goin' on down here."

Only Mohammed had remained with Rasheed. "Ain't no fight here," Mohammed said. "You see anybody fightin'?" he asked.

"Naw," Rasheed said. "Ain't no fight here." Shiny with perspiration and breathing as if he'd just run a five-minute mile, he stepped forward. "We just payin' our blood a little visit, is all. That ain't against the law, now is it?"

"Which of you boys lives on this street?" the black cop wanted to know.

"I do," said Jesse.

The cop gave him a quick once-over. "What're you doin' hangin' around with *this* bunch of losers?"

Shrugging innocently, Jesse said, "To each his own, I guess. . ."

"Say. . .ain't you Solon Turner's boy?" the cop asked.

Jesse nodded.

"I saw that article the *Business Journal* wrote about him. That picture of the two of you was nice. Real nice." He paused, then said, "I went to college with your daddy. He's a fine man. Fine." Through narrowed eyes, he scanned the crowd. "Does your daddy know about your. . .*friends*?"

Jesse shook his head. So far, Mr. Kim had kept his word and hadn't told Solon about the day Jesse had entered his shop, intent upon robbing him.

The gang stood a distance away, their sneering contempt filtering back to where Jesse, Rasheed, Mohammed, and the officers stood. "Get on out of here," the first cop hollered, "before I run you all in."

"Yeah?" Rasheed said. "What's the charge, *officer*?"

"I'll write you up for being ugly and dumb, for starters," he shot back. "And then we'll do a quick search of your pockets, and see what else we can add to the report."

Rasheed smirked, but started to saunter off, just the same, aware that the officers would find drugs, guns, ammo. . . "Now that we know where you live, Jester," Rasheed said, walking backwards, "we'll be back. . ."

Jesse's heart beat double time in response to the blatant threat. Up till now, his association with the gang had hurt no one but himself. Would Rasheed really come back some dark night. . .and harm Solon? Still, he couldn't let him see his fear. "We?" Jesse said. "I don't see any *we* around here."

Rasheed looked over his shoulder, and realized for the first time that he stood alone. "Shut up, fool," he said.

The Hispanic cop was already in the squad car when the black officer said, "If I see you with that bunch of trouble-makers again, I'm gonna have to have a little talk with your daddy, you hear?"

"Yessir," Jesse said.

"You think you'll be all right?" the cop asked.

Jesse raised his chin. "Yeah, I'll be okay." He glanced at the Bloods, who were driving off in a shiny black Olds-mobile, leaving a stunned and enraged Rasheed to find his own way back to the inner city.

"They've spent their whole lives blamin' others for bein' losers," he began. "They don't want to hear that a black man can pull himself up, out of the 'hood, and make something of himself with hard work and grit. . .like my dad." A small proud smile widened his mouth. "Besides, they're too busy sellin' crack and stealin' old ladies' purses to waste their time on me."

The policeman slid in behind the steering wheel, and as he pulled the driver's door shut, said, "How 'bout a ride home, son?"

His house was less than half a block away. "Why are you being so nice to me?"

"Because," the cop said, "I think you're worth it."

seven

"And so forty years of Baltimore history has ended today," the newscaster said, "as Wheedon Gardens crumbles to dust."

Jesse sat, mesmerized, by the slow-motion implosion that would level the project that had housed nearly five hundred residents. "That's the bomb," he said.

"No, dear," Faith pointed out, "the explosion experts are using dynamite, not bombs."

Rolling his eyes, Jesse grinned over his shoulder at Sadie's mother. "'The bomb,'" he explained patiently, "means 'boss.' 'Radical.'" Suddenly, a word she might identify with seemed to pop into his head, and he brightened. "'Cool!'" he said, a finger in the air.

Faith looked at Hannah. "Did you know about this?"

Her eldest daughter shrugged. "Sure, Mama." Winking at Jesse, she added, "But then, I'm 'boss,' too."

"Sadie?" Faith asked, hopeful her youngest daughter would side with her.

"The kids at Thornton have been saying that for over a year, Mama." She gave her mother a half smile. "Sorry. . ."

Solon was Faith's last hope. Crossing both arms over her chest, she raised her left brow. "I suppose you're all 'boss' and 'with it,' too. . ."

"The more things change," he said, "the more they stay the same. My mama thought 'cool' was outrageous."

Faith lifted the teacup and saucer from the polished cherry table beside her easy chair. After taking a dainty sip and replacing it on the hand-crocheted doily, she wrinkled up her face and said, "Well, *young'uns*, you might cut an old lady some slack." Resuming her former dignified voice, she straightened and added, "I thought I raised you better than that!"

Carleen giggled girlishly and covered her mouth with one hand. "Don't let 'em get to you, Grams." She glanced flirtatiously at Jesse. "They're not as 'boss' as they think they are."

Jesse raised his shoulders and his hands simultaneously, "Man, oh, man," he said, an innocent expression on his face, "I didn't mean to start an international incident."

There was a moment of silence, and then everyone began to laugh. "What did I tell you?" Solon asked Faith. "I'll bet you were saying that when you were a girl."

Faith raised her brows and her chin. "No. . .no. . .When I was a girl, we were still grunting in our caves."

"Good one, Grams," Cal Junior said when the second round of laughter died down. "Didn't know you had it in you."

The grandmother eyed her grandson lovingly. "Maybe, my darlin' boy, you don't know your old grandma as well as you think you do."

She punctuated her comment with a merry wink, then focused on the TV screen. "It's just sad to see a whole neighborhood go down," she snapped her fingers, "like that. Why, I remember when the city first built that place." Leaning against the headrest, her eyes fogged with a faraway look. "It was supposed to serve as a stopping place for folks who'd fallen on hard times. The idea, as I understood it, was to provide families with decent housing at an affordable rent, so they could save up and move on. . .to bigger, better things."

She sighed and shook her head. "Somehow, things got all twisted up; a family moved in, expecting life to improve. . ." Another sigh. "Where will all those good folks go now that their homes have been turned to rubble?"

"Paper says they're relocating to apartment complexes in the County," Hannah offered. "It's a big step up, if you ask me. . .Schools are better, there's less crime. . ."

"I suppose you're right," Faith conceded. "It just seems a shame. I feel so sorry for them. . ."

"Not me."

All eyes were on Solon.

"I lived there myself, for a time, when my daddy. . .he worked for the highway administration. . .broke his back. He was laid up nearly a year after that old fella lost control of his car and skidded into the road crew. Mama worked all sorts of hours, trying to make ends meet. But with six hungry mouths to feed. . ."

"Solon!" Faith interrupted. "I didn't know you had brothers and sisters! Why you been keepin' them a secret, boy?"

Chuckling, he leaned forward in his chair. "Don't you worry, Miss Faith, your daughter isn't dating a member of the Black Panthers or anything. The six I counted included my folks; Jesse was named for my oldest brother, who's a doctor at Chicago General. My younger brother, Samuel, lives in New York." Grinning, he said, "He likes us to tell folks he's a Broadway star. And my little sister moved to Lancaster with her husband a few years back; Eddie works for one of the biggest companies in the state of Pennsylvania."

"I guess it's hard, then, getting together when you're all so spread out around the country," Faith observed. "What about your mama and your daddy? Do they still live here in Baltimore?"

Leaning his elbows on his knees, Solon's grin faded. "Lost my father to a stroke nearly five years ago come December, and my mother had a fatal heart attack the very next spring."

"You lost your folks and your wife, all inside of three years?" Faith gasped. "You poor man! No wonder you. . ."

"Wasn't looking for pity, Miss Faith." Solon had clasped his hands together, and now he watched them open and close, open and close. "I only mentioned them to explain why I don't feel any pity for those folks," he said, pointing at the TV screen. "The minute the doctors let my daddy out of the hospital after that accident, he got back to work. Sold tools at

Sears for a time, managed a McDonald's restaurant for a while, even worked in the laundry down at Mercy Hospital. Minimum wage jobs, each and every one. He was smarter than that, and we all knew it; could have been president of a bank, or the head of a corporation with his business sense! But he never got the opportunity to further his education."

Solon's brow furrowed slightly as he admitted, "He always said, 'Long as my children and my wife have a roof over their heads and food in their bellies, I'll be a happy man.' Worked like a dog 'til the day he died, my daddy. If working hard doing menial labor wasn't too good for that great man, it's not too good for *those* folks," he growled, jabbing his forefinger in the air, indicating the people who had lived at Wheedon Gardens. "Unless they're infirm, what's their excuse for not doing an honest day's work?"

"Solon," Hannah said quietly, "a lot of the people at Wheedon Gardens are single mothers. Most of them can't afford to pay rent and day care, as well; that's why they're on the welfare roles."

He shook his head. "I realize it's not their fault. A woman can't be blamed if her man's not big enough to stick around and support the children he brings into this world. It's those husbands and fathers *I'm* talking about. Where did they get the idea life was some big game? Play 'til things get tough, then pick up your marbles and quit! How do they sleep nights, knowing their flesh and blood are suffering. . .hungry, cold, lonely. . .because of their self-centered, lazy. . ."

Suddenly, he stopped talking and scrubbed both hands over his face. "I'm sorry," he said quietly. "It's a subject I've never learned to discuss rationally; I ought to avoid discussing it at all, I suppose." He shrugged. "I just don't get it, that's all." Nodding toward the TV screen, he concluded his tirade. "If my daddy could do it with a broken back, *they* can do it. There's just no excuse good enough for all this whimpering."

He held up his hands in a gesture of helplessness. "That's it. I've said all I'm gonna say on *that* subject." Taking a deep breath, he grinned. "So," he said, clapping his hands together, "who's in the mood for pizza? My treat. . ."

Jesse, Carleen, and Cal Junior leapt to their feet and headed for the foyer. "Well," Jesse said, "what's everybody waiting for?" He opened the front door. "The three of us will sit in the back. Miss Hannah and Miss Faith, you'll get the backseat. . ." He smiled warmly at Sadie. "You ride shotgun, Miss Sadie."

He'd been calling her that for months now. She wasn't exactly sure when he'd dropped the more formal "Miss Burke," but Sadie's heart flipped each time he said her name. She knew no one could ever replace his mother, but maybe, if the Lord. . .and Solon. . .were so inclined, Jesse would have an opportunity to accept her as his stepmother. . .

❧

They sat around a big table at Pizza Hut, playfully arguing over whether they should order a pitcher of birch beer or cola. Solon solved the problem by asking the waitress to bring a pitcher of each. And when the friendly debate centered around deep dish or thin crust pizza, he told the girl to bring both.

The man was born to be a leader, Sadie observed. But by the time their salads arrived, as she watched him referee a squabble between Cal Junior and Carleen, she'd adjusted her opinion a mite: *Solon Turner was born to be a father.*

It seemed a shame, she thought, that ill health had prevented Coral from giving him but one child. Perhaps with siblings, Jesse would have adjusted to her death more quickly and easily; as the big brother, he'd likely have felt as duty bound to set an example for them as his father had been to be a model for Jesse.

On the other hand, the Lord knew exactly what He was doing: Jesse was so like Solon that, had he been expected to show younger brothers and sisters how to handle grief, he'd have kept them at arm's length to protect them from what he felt, thinking, as Solon had, it was the best and healthiest way.

Sighing, she sipped her birch beer and smiled at the warm,

family scene all around her. Faith had seated herself at one end of the rectangular table and had instructed Solon to take the other end. Hannah sat at Solon's left, and her children filled the chairs beside her. Jesse was at Solon's right, and Sadie next to him.

Sadie had been engaged in a lively discussion with Faith about what they would serve at their Thanksgiving Day get-together when she noticed Hannah and Solon, wearing somber expressions, whispering at the other end of the table. "Turkey and cranberry sauce, naturally," Faith was saying; "anything else would be un-American! But I insist on serving my candied ham, too. Hannah will make her sweet potatoes, of course, and you'll whip up your scrumptious baked beans. . ."

Faith saw that her words were falling on deaf ears, and she ceased speaking. Leaning in close, she whispered, "What do you make of that?"

Without taking her eyes from Solon and Hannah, Sadie whispered back, "I honestly don't know." She met her mother's eyes then. "You don't suppose she's telling him where to find those snapshots you took when I was a toddler. . ."

Faith giggled. "You mean the 'baby in the bathtub' pictures? If I were you, I'd say a prayer, right this minute, that your sister is telling some *other* secret on you! If he finds out what a scrawny thing you were, he'll never pop the question, 'cause he'll believe all the babies you give him will be just as bony!"

"Mama, I'm shocked to find out how you really felt. You always told me I was the most beautiful baby ever born!"

"Oh, Sadie," Faith said. "Sometimes you can be so gullible. I said the same thing to Hannah. . .and she reminded me of a little tomato worm when she was born, what with her round little head and those two sprigs of hair standin' up on either side of her face. . ."

Their laughter drew the attention of everyone else at the table. . .including Solon and Hannah. Their expressions brightened a bit in response to the happy interruption. "What's so funny?" Hannah wanted to know. "Do I have a tomato skin between my teeth or. . ."

At the mention of the vegetable, Sadie and Faith laughed harder than ever, much to Hannah's dismay. "I think maybe it's time Sadie and I changed seats, Solon," she said through her teeth. "Seems my little sister is missing you so much, she's taken to filling the gap at my expense."

Sadie met Solon's eyes as her sister rose to trade places. He, too, was smiling, but the grin never made it to his eyes. He quirked an eyebrow, telling her wordlessly that Hannah's glee was about as genuine as the crystal candle holder in the center of their table. A strange mix of emotions pulsed inside her. . .joy at merely being in his presence, pride that he'd so quickly bonded with her family, pleasure that Hannah felt she could share her secret with him, gratitude that he'd listened with such sincere interest. She almost proved that gratitude by rushing to trade places with her sister and then pressing a kiss to his dark, rugged cheek! But something made her stay in her own seat.

If Hannah continued to sit beside him, perhaps she'd finish telling Solon about whatever had been troubling her. She'd certainly not shared her concerns with Faith or Sadie. . .a fact mother and daughter had discussed at length that very morning. "Stay right where you are, sister dear," Sadie instructed, grinning at Solon. "The view is much better from here. Besides," she added with a wave of her hand, "Mama and I are. . .bonding. . ."

The statement inspired another round of laughter, and by the time it blended with the din of quiet conversation, Hannah had taken her seat again. And, just as Sadie had hoped, in a matter of minutes, the whispering had begun again.

"I can't *wait* to get her alone and find out what all the hush-hush talk is about," Faith said quietly.

"Well," Sadie returned, smiling lovingly at Solon, "if you don't call me at work first thing in the morning and tell me what you've learned, I promise never to tell you what I find out!"

"She might swear me to secrecy," Faith warned.

"That's never stopped you before."

She shrugged nonchalantly. "True enough. Still. . ."

Sadie gave her mother a sideways hug. "I love you from here to California, Mama," she said, planting a kiss on her cinnamon-brown cheek, "but you reap what you sow. . . ."

Grinning slyly, Faith lifted her red plastic glass of cola. "Never thought I'd see the day when a daughter of mine would threaten me."

Giggling, Sadie said affectionately, "But Mama, it's not a threat. . .it's a promise."

ॐ

"She's afraid," Solon said, "and who can blame her?"

Sadie didn't know what to say, so she said nothing.

Solon took her hand. "Don't worry, sweetie. She's a strong woman; she's survived far worse than this, don't forget."

She exhaled a deep breath. "I know. But it just seems so unfair." Facing him, she blinked up into his eyes. "Hannah is a good woman, Solon. She deserves better than this."

He nodded. "There's no denying that. But you can't fight city hall."

Scowling, she shook her head. "It isn't as if Hannah and the other KinderKare employees are the only ones affected by the budget cuts. If they close down that day care center, where will those children go? What will their mothers do?"

"I don't mean to sound like a pompous old man, but I've learned that things generally have a way of turning themselves around. Take Jesse, for example." He lifted her chin on a bent forefinger. "A year ago, I'd have written him off as a lost cause. And then you came along, and won him over with nothing but the warmth of your smile and the strength of your faith in him."

She hung her head. "You give me too much credit. I only did my job." She met his eyes again. "It was you who made the difference. Your time and attention and love."

"He deserved to have that in the first place." Now it was his turn to scowl. "Call it what you will—stubborn pride, know-it-all attitude—my way wasn't working." He looked deep into her eyes. "If it hadn't been for you, I'd never have seen. . ."

"Yes, you would," she interrupted, laying her fingertips over his lips. "Eventually, your love for him would have put your back to the wall. You might have gone about it differently if I hadn't been in the picture, but the results would have been the same."

He grinned crookedly. "You really have that much confidence in me?"

She nodded. "I really do. You're a wonderful father, Solon. The only sad fact in all this is that you didn't have the opportunity to shower your love on a whole passel of kids."

If he hadn't kissed her just then, Solon would have admitted that he'd been thinking the same thing, practically from the moment he'd first set eyes on her. He'd gone over it again and again in his mind, had prayed about it, too. But he'd only known her since February. . .not even a full year yet. . .Shaking his head, he wondered how a grown man—a man who owned a successful company—could go and do something so foolish as to fall in love so quickly!

He'd always prided himself on being a detail man. He read between every line, looked around every corner. No stone went unturned; he never allowed a single thing to fall through the cracks. When plans were laid down in front of him, he traced every stroke of the architect's pen as though it were a treasure map rather than a set of blueprints. Likewise, when a budget was placed on his desk, he studied every square inch of it.

Solon knew something about taking the measure of a person, too, and took hiring and firing employees no less seriously. He liked to think that, over the years, he'd developed a knack for selecting the construction industry's most elite personnel.

In this business, snap decisions could make or break a job, and he'd had to learn how to quickly size up a situation. . .or an individual. He hadn't taken more than a couple of months to identify Joey Mulhearne's best traits. Hadn't taken twenty weeks to realize the Hunt Club project would put him front and center in the building trade.

Why was he so surprised at his feelings for Sadie? He'd looked even more closely and carefully at her character than he'd looked at Coral's. Not once, not in all the months he'd known her, had Sadie given him reason to suspect she was anything but what she appeared to be. So maybe he hadn't known her such a short time after all.

So what are you waiting for, man? he asked himself. *Tell her how you feel*!

Solon was waiting, frankly, because he'd nearly lost Jesse. Now that he had him back, he wouldn't risk losing him again. Not even for Sadie.

Now that he'd reclaimed his faith in God, he knew it was time he got on his knees and prayed for divine guidance. He'd been a devout man. . .before Coral's death. Reared by faithful followers, Solon had rarely missed a Sunday service, read the Bible daily, said morning and evening devotions, even sang in the gospel choir.

The morning after his wedding, he'd left his sleeping bride alone in their honeymoon hotel to walk along the beach in Ocean City, where he praised the Creator. Home again, he and Coral worked hard, and saved every cent, and within that first year, they had put a down payment on their very first home. They had a solid roof overhead, plenty of food in the Frigidaire, and heat in the furnace. And he had praised God.

Just when he'd convinced himself life couldn't get any better, Jesse came into the world, long-toed little feet kicking, pudgy fists bunched, hollering like a miniature James Brown. Gathering his infant son in his arms, Solon had cried tears of pure joy, and thanked the Almighty for yet another blessing. Jesse thrived, and so did the business, and Solon knew exactly Who to thank.

But Coral's illness changed all that. If God could truly read men's hearts, surely he knew that Solon would have traded everything he'd earned, and everything he hoped to be—the respect of his peers, the business, the house. . .to have her well again. But God seemed to have turned a deaf ear to his prayers. Coral's health continued to decline, despite Solon's fervent prayers.

He'd always believed in the power of positive thinking; if you could dream it, it was possible. But in Solon's mind, the gates of heaven slammed shut on the day she died. If God couldn't be bothered to answer his heartfelt plea—especially since it was more for Coral and Jesse than for himself, then for a long time he'd felt he couldn't be bothered to waste his time in the asking!

Now, he was learning to praise God again. But a part of him was still afraid—afraid that God would bless him again, only to demand that Solon give up his happiness all over again. I'm just plum scared to walk by faith. . .

But Sadie was the woman for him; he was certain of it. The question: How would he let *her* know it?

eight

Sadie had gone all out for Thanksgiving, decorating the fence, the lamp posts, even the mailbox with brown and gold silk flowers, Indian corn, and pumpkins. She had cleaned and shined the house from top to bottom, and filled it with the delicious scents of baking pies and breads and cookies. It had been hard work, but the more she toiled, the more she was filled with exhilaration rather than exhaustion. *Must be a labor of love*, she'd smiled to herself.

As promised, Faith carefully decorated a huge ham with pineapple and cloves and candy glaze. Hannah came early in the morning on Thanksgiving Day and shimmied a pan of sweet potatoes and brown sugar into the oven, between the ham and the turkey. Sadie's baked beans had been bubbling in the crock pot since early that morning. The kitchen counter was lined with pies, a three-tier fudge-iced cake, and several baskets overflowing with sweet rolls and date bread.

The good silver had been lovingly polished and Grandma's linen tablecloth was laundered and pressed. The only thing missing were guests with healthy appetites. . .And a little sunshine.

The best-laid plans of mice and wo-*men*, Sadie mused, pouting as she stared dismally through the downpour that pelted the kitchen window, melting the silk flowers she'd taped to the fence. She watched the rain turn to sleet and then snow; sighing, she reached for the portable phone. No sense making everyone come out in such miserable weather. . .

"Hello. . ."

"Hi, Jesse. It's Sadie."

"Hey! How you doin'?"

"*I'm* fine," she said. "Too bad the weather isn't. . ." She paused, then, "Is your dad there?"

"Sure. Hold on, I'll get him."

Sadie winced as the boy bellowed, "Da-a-ad! It's for you!"

Soon, she heard the recognizable click that told her he'd picked up an extension phone. "Hello?"

"Solon. . .good morning."

"Good morning to you, too," he said. Then, "I've got it, Jess, thanks. You can hang up now."

"Aw-w-w," the boy complained. "You mean I can't stay on the line and listen to you guys talk mushy?"

"'Fraid not, son. Knowing you were listening would only cramp my style."

Sadie could hear the smile in his voice when Jesse said, "Harumph. Didn't know you *had* a style," and hung up.

"What can I do for you?" Solon asked. "Not that you need a reason to brighten my day. . ."

Sadie sighed into the receiver. "Well, I'm sure you've looked outside. It's such an ugly day! The roads must be a mess."

"It's gonna take more than a little wind and ice to dampen *our* Thanksgiving. We have too much to be thankful for this year."

"But I just heard on the radio that the police are advising people to stay off the roads and. . ."

Solon chuckled softly. "Now, don't get your socks in a knot. The day's not a total loss. . ."

". . .yet."

He assumed a paternal, scolding tone. "Why, Sadie Burke, I don't believe I've ever heard you sound so downhearted. You've got to think positively."

"But the weather report says. . ."

". . .that it's going to rain, sleet, and snow for days." He chuckled. "I watch TV, too, y'know."

"You and Jesse are welcome to come, anyway, of course. . . because if you don't, I have no idea what Mama and I will do with all this food. . .but I won't blame you a bit if you'd rather not come out in this rotten weather."

"I own a four-wheeler. I can maneuver through rain and snow and dark of night."

She giggled. "You're not a part-time mailman, are you?"

Laughing, Solon said, "You've gotta be kiddin'! I don't even own an Uzi!"

"Oh, Solon," she said softly, "you're so good-natured. I'm sorry that I'm being such a baby about this. It's just that Thanksgiving has always been one of my favorite holidays. I *love* having the family all gathered together. I'm sorry if I've been sounding like a baby."

His voice grew deeper and quieter. "No need to apologize, Sadie. I know a little something about disappointment, myself." He brightened slightly to add, "Now, what time should we be there?"

How self-centered and immature she must have sounded. How self-centered and immature she was behaving! Of course Solon was right. They still had so much to be thankful for! "I'm sorry," she said again, "and this time, I mean it." She took a deep breath. "Be here at one, and *please*, don't bring anything to eat! And drive carefully."

"Okay," he said. "One o'clock, empty-handed."

❧

Carleen and Jesse had been sitting in the enclosed porch of the row house for nearly an hour, chatting and listening to the music filtering in from the CD player in Sadie's parlor. "I don't know what grown-ups like about jazz," Jesse observed. "It's so. . .It's so depressing and. . .and *noisy*."

"It's not so bad. Some of it *is* kind of sad, but it can be very happy music, too." She crossed her ankles, stared straight ahead. "Jesse. . .can I ask you something?"

"Sure," he agreed, nodding.

"Why do you hang around with Rasheed and those. . ."

"I don't hang around with them."

She turned slightly on the sofa to face him. "I've seen you with them, Jesse." Impetuously, Carleen grabbed his hand.

The look on her face reminded him of Sadie when she was doling out motherly advice, making Carleen seem, for the moment, far older than her thirteen years.

"Don't you know who they *are*. . .*what* they are?"

Her expression, her tone, her attitude, hurt him. He liked Carleen, and he had a small hope hidden deep inside him that someday, perhaps, they'd be more than just friends. The disappointment she so obviously felt cut him to the core. Unable to face her, he focused on their hands, linked in friendship on her lap. He had done the right thing, and severed all ties with the Bloods. If she hadn't seen that. . .

He wanted to ask who she thought she was. What gave her the right to sound so superior? But Jesse said nothing and asked nothing. She, like he, was one parent shy of a full load. Her father had left her, just as surely as his mother had died. But Carleen hadn't let herself get all out of control. Instead, she'd done the exact opposite. Still, her smug superior demeanor was beginning to rile him slightly. She might have chosen to handle her problems differently, but how superior was she *really*, if she was capable of making him feel this small?

"You can pout and frown and give me the silent treatment all you want, Jesse Turner. It won't change the fact that the Bloods are a gang. They rob people and sell drugs, and. . ." She looked around to ensure their privacy, then, satisfied they were alone, whispered, "I heard they raped a girl last week."

He'd heard the same thing. According to the rumor, the Bloods had grabbed a former classmate from the Reisterstown Mall parking lot, pulled her into a windowless panel van, and drove off. Kenitra had quit school the previous year, and those who knew her knew, too, that she'd taken to the streets, where she did whatever it took to supply her crack cocaine habit. Drugs had so numbed her mind and body that it wouldn't have been necessary to haul Kenitra into that van. The Bloods had forced her. . .because for them, it had been some sick and sordid sort of game.

The police found her miles from the shopping center, muttering and dazed, unable to explain where she'd been. . .or what had happened to her. The rumor was that she hadn't spoken since that awful night.

He'd known from the start that the Bloods were trouble. Big trouble. What had made him get involved with them in the first place was as much a mystery to Jesse as anyone else. Sadie, in what he called "counselor talk," had explained that he'd been angry with the world from the moment he'd learned about his mother's illness. His outrageous behavior, Sadie said, had been Jesse's misguided way of taking control of his out-of-control life. She compared his actions to those of anorexics and bullemics, for whom food—what they'd eat, how much they'd eat, *whether* they'd eat—became their way of expressing that they were in command of *some* facet of their lives. In Jesse's case, breaking the rules was another way of saying, "I'm in charge of *this*, at least."

Others in her line of work had said similar things, but Jesse hadn't really listened to a word of their advice. Handing down their advice in imperious voices as they regarded him with their arrogant stares, the psychologists and psychiatrists his father had hired represented yet another area of his life over which Jesse had no control. "Your problems," they'd maintained, "stem from your refusal to deal with your mother's death; until and unless you come to grips with the inevitable, there's little chance for improvement."

Improvement! Jesse had thought. I *don't need to improve*, you do! If they were so smart, why didn't they know that he *had* dealt with his mother's death: She was gone for good, and he missed her, and there was absolutely nothing he could do about that.

Sadie's patient prodding had made him admit the truth in what the other counselors had said. Without the judgmental manner of those who came before her, she'd encouraged him to dig deep and ask himself some tough questions. Not once had she made him feel stupid or childish or foolish when the answers weren't "textbook" enough.

Once she'd forced him, in her sweet and gentle way, to admit his own part in his life gone wrong, the wisdom of George Green, Mr. Kim, and even Principal Johnson, began to make sense. He'd weighed their guidance—and the reasons they'd given it—and began to assess the reasons for his surly behavior.

The self-evaluation required more than an admission of how he'd been living these past few years; it demanded that Jesse make the decisions and take the steps that would alter his life course. He'd made those decisions and had begun taking those steps.

His relationship with teachers, coaches, and especially Solon had never been better. His report cards had gone from failing grades to above-average scores, because he'd *gone* to school and done the work that had been expected of him.

The boys and girls who had been his friends before Coral's death had started calling and dropping by the house again. He couldn't remember the last time he'd been with Rasheed and the Bloods.

But wait. . .yes. He could. That day near his house, when the whole bunch of them had descended on his neighborhood. . .Despite the fact that he hadn't seen or heard from any of them in weeks, Jesse couldn't escape the horrifying thought that sooner or later, he'd be asked to pay the price for his brief association with them. Maybe, though, God would smile upon him, and turn his brave speech to the cop that day into reality. . .

How long he'd been sitting there beside Carleen, day-dreaming about his past—and his future—Jesse didn't know. Difficult as it was, he forced himself to meet her eyes. "I was a fool to have anything to do with them. If I could go back and change things, I would."

Carleen frowned and shook her head. "Seems a boy with any sense would have figured out what they were *before* he got involved with them." She pressed her lips together primly. "I'm not sure I even want to be friends with a boy who could be that stupid."

He scowled. "Man, oh, man, Carleen," he bit out. "Ain't it enough I admitted my mistake? Ain't it enough I'm doin' what I ought to now?" He sighed. "Sounds like you're saying I'm not even allowed to make any mistakes in the first place."

She pursed her lips, then said, "The Lord Jesus didn't cozy up to the money changers in the temple before He threw them out. . ."

Exasperated, Jesse blew a stream of air through his teeth. "Yeah? Well, I never claimed to be no Lord Jesus. And by the way, didn't He also say, 'Let he who is without sin cast the first stone.'" He glared at her. "You telling me you never made a mistake, Carleen? You saying you've never done anything you wish you hadn't?"

Carleen's eyes widened as she sat in stunned silence. For as long as he'd known her, she'd never been at a loss for words. "What's the matter, Carleen?" he pressed. "You seemed to have plenty to say a minute ago." Narrowing his eyes, he added, "What have you got to say to *that*? And how do you *know* so much about the Bloods, anyway? Maybe you've done more than look at 'em; maybe you've seen 'em up close and personal. . ."

Understanding his implication, Carleen gasped. "I have eyes and ears," she snapped as she snatched her hand away. "Just because I work hard in school to get good grades doesn't mean I don't know the score. Just because I don't like to run around with criminals and worry my mother, and do things that could get me sent to the. . ."

As though she'd suddenly become aware of the wrath in her voice, Carleen stopped talking.

Jesse gave her a tight smile. "Go ahead. Say it. 'The Thornton School.'" He wanted to tell her he'd cleaned up his act, that the fact he was back at Bradley proved it. But what was the point? She'd believe what she wanted to believe about him, no matter what he said.

Much about their backgrounds should have made them compatible. They'd both been raised, these past years, by single parents who had struggled night and day, year in and year out, doing without their own comforts to see to it that their children would grow up in a nice house, in a decent neighborhood. He'd certainly never gone to bed hungry, and Jesse doubted Carleen had ever felt the pangs of an empty stomach, either. His clothes were clean and in style. . .and so were hers. And both of their parents had made clear that each child would graduate not only from high school, but college as well.

All these things should have given them a lot in common, but Jesse suddenly realized that Carleen didn't have a clue who he was and what he was trying to do with his life. Worse, she didn't seem to care. Her only interest, he believed, was making the comparisons that put her in the bright light, and he in the shadows.

For a long time—up to this very moment, in fact—he'd thought Carleen was superior to him. But Jesse had survived a gauntlet, and that very survival had made him question many things. Jesse would have told her all this, if not for his respect for her mother, her grandma, and her aunt. *Wouldn't it amaze her*, Jesse asked himself, *to know that I see how much* she *has in common with Rasheed*. . .

Rasheed had prejudged him—presuming he'd follow every order, no questions asked, like every other Blood—just as Carleen had been prejudging him in her own prissy, arrogant way. After all, it didn't take a genius to see that Rasheed and the Bloods were the underbelly of society. That Carleen had defined them as bad news didn't make her superior to him!

Admittedly, he'd considered doing some pretty awful things at Rasheed's request. But he hadn't! He'd condemned their activities, but *not* from some lofty self-righteous perch. He'd given Rasheed a chance to prove himself. If Carleen was such an all-fired good Christian girl, why couldn't she give him the same understanding he'd given the leader of the murderous, thieving gang?

Jesse stood and slowly walked into the other room.

"So, when do you want to go?"

He stopped, and looked over his shoulder at her. "Huh?"

"I thought you said you wanted to go for a walk later."

You've got a lot to learn about being a friend, Carleen, he thought, shaking his head. He might have never made the connection if he hadn't listened to the grocer, the janitor, the principal, the counselor. Their advice had taught him that nothing was what it appeared to be, and if he hadn't accepted that, he'd have continued to grow farther from Solon. . .and more and more like Rasheed.

He wouldn't have wished upon anyone the agony of his strife-wrought life of late, least of all Carleen. But friendship requires a person to accept others as they are, even while gently urging them to be the best they can be. Being Carleen's friend might require acceptance of her, but it most certainly did not demand that he totally overlook—what had Pastor Higgins called it?—her "holier-than-thou attitude."

Yes, as far as Jesse was concerned, Carleen and Rasheed had that, at least, in common. They thought they were better than the rest of the world.

"So. . .when are we leaving?" She grinned flirtatiously.

Jesse sighed. Suddenly, from where she'd positioned herself, high on her self-made pedestal, she didn't look quite so pretty, quite so perfect. He wondered what he'd seen in her in the first place. "You don't want to go for a walk with a fool like me, Carleen," he said quietly. "Why don't you find somebody who deserves you." Mentally, he invited her to pay particular attention to the word "deserves."

His words seemed to have paralyzed her, and Carleen sat, stone still and silent, as he ambled into the other room. *Maybe someone else would like to go for a walk with me,* he thought.

❧

Rasheed had always believed he might have been a good

student if he'd stayed in school, and now, he had proof. One of his last assignments before dropping out had been to read *Mutiny on the Bounty*. He'd never cracked the book, of course, but his classmates had, and Rasheed remembered still the lively discussions that had gone on all around him as he pretended boredom and disgust with their eager enthusiasm. Now he believed he knew exactly how the ship's captain must have felt when the uprising began.

For Rasheed, the revolt started on the day he'd led the gang into Jesse's neighborhood. Rasheed was a lion, the dominant male, and the Bloods were his pride. From the moment he'd created them, anyone who hoped to take away his pride would *have* to be another dominant figure. Another swaggering, bullying lion as bad—or worse—than he was.

But now, the Bloods were crumbling around him, because of an introspective, soft-spoken rich man's boy, and Rasheed couldn't believe it! Certainly other kids had tried to defend themselves against his might and fury, but not one had succeeded. This one, this Jesse Turner, had something none of the others had had, and Rasheed's hatred of him bubbled and surged within him like a cauldron of poisonous witches' brew.

He recalled the rush of adrenaline when they'd first stepped out into the clearing to let Jesse know they'd arrived. . .in his very own safe little world. Fear had widened Jesse's near-black eyes and his shoulders had hunched with tension. *Oh, but he's a cool one*, Rasheed had thought. Instinct, more than anything else, had made him aware of Jesse's anxiety; like a lion that smells its victim's terror, he'd recognized Jesse's quavering voice and trembling lips as symptoms of dread. And like a scared rabbit, trapped in his burrow, Jesse's pupils dilated as he stared into the face of a hungry predator.

Still. . .despite the horror he no doubt knew he'd face, Jesse had squared his shoulders, lifted his chin, and stuffed his shaky hands deep into his pockets. Rasheed remembered resisting the urge to laugh at the boy's feeble attempt to mask his concern.

Even when he'd spelled out why the Bloods were there, in language any fool could understand, Jesse hadn't backed down. That, frankly, had surprised him, for Rasheed had fully expected the spoiled little rich boy to turn tail and barricade himself behind that big oak door on his fancy house.

But Jesse hadn't run. Quite the opposite. From somewhere deep inside him, he'd summoned the courage and the strength to face his opponent. *And he* knows *I'm his enemy,* Rasheed thought now, as he'd thought then.

The same instinctual perceptions that had always enabled him to know when to strike had told him Jesse's bravado was nothing but a disguise. Nothing in Rasheed's experience helped him understand why Jesse had confronted the Bloods in that defiant, determined way. *Fool was* scared, Rasheed told himself for the hundredth time. *That's why he didn't run . . .he couldn't run!*

Rasheed slammed his fist onto the kitchen counter. The hollow echo of his flesh meeting the cold hard tile reminded him exactly how alone he was. How alone he'd been since. . .

He growled under his breath as he slid the TV dinner into the microwave. His stomach growled nearly as loudly, protesting almost twenty-four hours without a meal. Rasheed was accustomed to having food brought to him by his minions, but none had come last night, nor the following morning. Thanksgiving Day, and he was all alone. Not that Thanksgiving meant anything to him. . .

Flopping onto the recliner end of his long, white leather sofa, he balanced the cardboard tray on his lap and stirred the macaroni and cheese. *Where'd you go wrong*? he asked himself, popping a forkful of pasta and sauce into his mouth.

But Rasheed already knew the answer. It had been gnawing at him since Jesse threw that first punch. . .

His mistake, Rasheed admitted, had been in ignoring his own inner warning. He'd known from the moment Jesse had refused to back down on the basketball court that this was no ordinary competitor. Made from a slightly different mold,

Jesse was precisely the kind of kid who could take over as leader of the Bloods, much in the same way a young lion will fight for dominion over the pride. Only in this case, the victory wouldn't go to the biggest or the strongest. Rather, it would be the *smartest* animal who'd triumph.

As he scraped the last of the cheese sauce from the corners of the square plate, he conceded the obvious: Jesse Turner was someone to be reckoned with. If he'd recognized that earlier, he'd still have total control over the Bloods. As it was, only half of them did as they were told; even his own brother listened only when he felt like it. Witnessing his shame—to be felled by the shorter, thinner Jesse—had been all the evidence they'd needed to question his leadership skills, to doubt his ability to lead.

Rasheed looked around the well-appointed apartment and listened to the sounds emanating from the TV's huge speakers. The only voices in the room came from within the set, and with every reverberated word, he was reminded again of his solitary status.

Before Jesse Turner had stumbled into his life, Rasheed had had it all. What made it all seem so appetizing was that *others* knew it, too. He was a self-made man at the age of fifteen. How many other kids could boast *that*?

Jesse Turner had, in a mere matter of months, crippled all he'd built these past four years. With nothing more than a defiant glare and an upraised fist, he'd toppled Rasheed Potts and his mini-empire. *How'd the fool do that?* he demanded silently. The leader of the Bloods had interpreted the boy's sometimes soft-spoken, trembling voice as signs of weakness; he'd failed to see the quiet confidence and strength that had always been there in the younger, smaller boy. . .and was only now beginning to show itself.

Hindsight is twenty-twenty. He had no idea who'd penned the cliché!, but Rasheed thought it made good sense. . . especially now. Unlike Jesse, Rasheed had never known the unconditional love of a father or a mother and, unlike Jesse, he'd never lived in a nice house in a decent neighborhood, and Rasheed hated Jesse for being different from himself.

Still. . .his hard, lonely life had taught him a thing or two about survival in the jungle. Stubborn determination and ruthless ambition had provided him with other things. Being the man in charge meant he could have a foxy lady at his side any time he snapped his fingers. Take this apartment, for example, and the gleaming black Olds parked at the curb. "No rich old man gave me *any* of it," he muttered bitterly.

With one lucky punch, Jesse had taken more than Rasheed's control over the Bloods, he'd humiliated the leader in front of his only family, his *pride*. To win back that control and their respect he'd have to do more than take Jesse down. . .

"Gotta take this fool *out*," he growled, glowering.

nine

Solon slouched on the sofa, thumbs hooked through his belt loops, head lolling to one side, and groaned. "I'm full as a tick. If I keep eating like that, I'll weigh three hundred pounds by next Thanksgiving."

Giggling, Sadie snuggled closer beside him and patted his stomach. Leaning her head on his shoulder, she said, "There's no rule that says you have to eat three slices of pumpkin pie. . ."

"Can I help it if your mama is Baltimore's best baker?"

She stretched languorously. "I'm as contented as a Carnation cow. I believe I could sit here beside you, just like this, until Christmas." Stifling a yawn, she said, "But this isn't getting those dishes done."

He kissed her temple. "May I remind you that there wasn't a person at the table who didn't offer to help. You should have taken them up on it while you had the chance. Now they're all gone and. . ."

Sadie scooted to the edge of the sofa cushions and poked a finger into his food-filled tummy. "They're not *all* gone," she said, one hand on her hip as she stood, then extended the other hand toward him.

Solon looked left and right, as if to say, who, me? Meeting her smiling eyes again, he took a deep breath and heaved himself up from the sofa. "Well," he said, taking her hand, "I suppose the sooner we get that mess cleaned up, the sooner I can have your undivided attention." He wiggled his eyebrows suggestively. "Because the others will be back from their walk before too long. . ."

She knew Solon was right; soon they'd all be back, chattering like magpies. Sadie headed for the kitchen.

"Wait," he said, grabbing her wrist. "Show me that you'll miss me when I go home."

Grinning, she said, "Solon, this isn't getting those dishes. . ."

Solon closed his eyes and pointed at his puckered his lips, then began mimicking a goldfish. Laughing softly, Sadie pressed her lips to his.

When the long-lasting kiss ended, he said, "Doesn't look to me like you're going to miss me very much."

Hands on her hips, Sadie considered the challenge. She stepped up to him, sent a wait-'til-you-see-this look on the invisible thread of passion that now connected them, and kissed him again.

"Man," he sighed when she stepped back. "I was wrong. You're gonna miss me, all right. . ." He stood there, silent and staring for a moment, his eyes still blazing from the heat of her kiss. "You're gonna miss me," he asked, his voice a near whisper, "but why?"

There was but one answer, and Sadie gave it. "Because I love you."

She had much to be grateful for, and she'd admitted it aloud earlier, as the Burke family tradition of listing things they were thankful for worked its way around the table.

"I thank the good Lord for preserving this old body, and not giving it too many aches and pains," Faith had said. "But mostly, I thank Him for all of you."

Solon mentioned his business, his son's success, and, smiling at Sadie, his newfound happiness. Jesse, in turn, acknowledged his appreciation for all the caring people who had made his achievements possible in the first place. Hannah thanked God for her two wonderful, healthy children. . .and for Floyd. . .who'd slipped a diamond ring on the third finger of her left hand that morning as he helped her carry pans of food out to her car. Carleen had primly given thanks for good health and good grades. Cal Junior, smacking his lips as he regarded the meal, clapped his hands together and said that he, for one, was grateful for good food.

Even as she laughed at her nephew's joke, Sadie met Solon's eyes. "I'm thankful for you," she'd said softly, and then turning to the others she'd added, "for all of you."

After that, saying she loved him had seemed easy and natural. But not nearly as natural as hearing him say it right back. And when he added, "Will you marry me, Sadie?" she gave him the answer that naturally came to her lips.

"Yes."

❧

The next day, Jesse went to a friend's house to work on a project that was due after Thanksgiving vacation. He had already worked hard on his half of the project, spending countless hours in the library, and even more time at home, poring over the books on the shelves in his living room. Troy had done his fair share, too. Between them, the boys believed, they'd earned a solid A.

He was sauntering home from Troy's house, hands in his pockets as he rehearsed the way he'd introduce the subject in school first thing Monday morning. Grinning, Jesse wished the principal could be present to hear him announce that he and Troy had chosen one of the most difficult biology experiments on the science teacher's list. Re-creating a steam engine had been no easy feat, but they'd done it, and done it well!

November's early dark was settling over the streets, and a cold moon peeked over the roofs of the houses. Jesse walked a little faster, eager to be inside his warm house. As he turned the corner and headed up his own street, a huge figure stepped out from the shadows and blocked his path. Within seconds, two, three, four more phantom figures flanked it.

"Where you think you goin', schoolboy?" Rasheed demanded, flexing his fists.

Frowning, Jesse stopped and considered his options. He could run, and might even outdistance the bigger, bulkier boy. But by the time he fumbled with the screen door and the inside doorknob, Rasheed would be on him. Jesse didn't want whatever the gang leader had planned for him to happen on his own front porch.

Or he could fight. Bravado had worked with this bunch before. . ."What's wrong, Rasheed. . . you bored? Couldn't find some poor old lady to torment, or a little kid to terrify?"

Rasheed's upper lip pulled back in a menacing scowl. "Go ahead, *fool*, make jokes. . .while you can. . ."

Jesse shook his head. "Why am I wasting time talking to you?" he asked, attempting to go around him.

Rasheed, it seemed, had anticipated this, and he took a long sideways step, barring Jesse's path yet again. "You ain't goin' nowhere but *down*, Jester," he hissed. Mohammed and two other Bloods stood their ground, arms crossed over their chests, looking, in the silvery glow of the moon, like three pewter Mr. Cleans.

The sight might have inspired a chuckle, or at the very least a grin, if Jesse hadn't caught sight of Rasheed's right arm, bending at an awkward angle as he reached around behind himself. In an eye blink, he'd withdrawn the pistol tucked into his belt, and aimed it directly at Jesse.

In the short time Jesse had been involved with the Bloods, he had seen a few handguns. But nothing like this one. It was dull-black, bulky, and reminded him of the weapon Clint Eastwood had so blatantly flaunted in the movie *Dirty Harry*—and it was big enough to make Jesse realize its destructive power. He might have tried to flee then. . .if he could have made his feet move. Frozen with fear, Jesse couldn't seem to take his eyes off the square-cut barrel.

There was no time to wonder what he'd ever done to inspire Rasheed to point a gun at his chest. He'd heard stories about gang members who hunted down boys who'd thought better of joining, but surely. . .

"Say your prayers, fool," Rasheed growled.

Something told him he was going to need prayers. Lots of them. But even before Jesse had a chance to search his mind for one, instinct forced him to raise his hands in a gesture of helpless supplication, and turn his head to protect his eyes from the flare of bright white light that flashed from the muzzle.

He'd heard the sound hundreds, thousands of times, maybe, on TV, in the movie theater. None of it had prepared him for the ear-blasting, rib-wracking explosion that cracked the quiet night. Nothing could have prepared him for the pain, either.

Again, instinct took over. In one smooth move, Jesse clutched both hands to his chest and slumped slowly, slowly, into a crumpled heap onto the grass near the curb. He closed his eyes and held his breath, hoping to stanch the searing, aching agony that pulsed in the upper-left quadrant of his chest. He wasn't dead, he realized, not yet. But if Rasheed thought he was. . .

As though some invisible, powerful force had put its controlling finger on his life's rewind button, pictures flashed through Jesse's mind: Coral and Solon. Faith and Hannah. And Sadie. He would miss them all so much. . .

Ever since he'd first learned to swim, Jesse had been amazed and intrigued by the strange, pulsing sound the world took on when he chose to dive beneath the water's surface. The world sounded that way now as he lay there, breathing so shallowly that his chest barely moved at all. From what seemed to Jesse the end of a mile-long tunnel, he heard the foggy, groggy voice of Rasheed Potts. "Fool ain't laughin' now, is he?" the leader said to his gang. "*Now* you know who is the baddest Blood."

He turned toward his brother, his mouth wide with a triumphant grin, but Mohammed only scowled.

"What you lookin' at?" Rasheed demanded.

Mohammed gave a disgusted shrug. "We only came 'cause you said we'd see a good fight." He nodded at Jesse's still body. "You think this is a good fight? You think you bad 'cause you iced a schoolboy?"

Rasheed grimaced. "You give me anymore lip," he said, waving the gun in the air, "I'll *ice* you."

A look that mingled disgust with contempt crossed Mohammed's face as he gave the weapon a cursory glance.

A siren wailed, a faraway, pitiful plea that grew louder and more insistent with every tick of Jesse's watch. As the noise neared, he listened to the sounds of footsteps, at first so close he worried one might land upon his bloody chest, then dimming and diminishing until he heard nothing, nothing at all.

❧

Solon wrapped his arms around Sadie and pressed her close against him. "You think I should tell him alone, or should we talk to him together?"

Standing on tiptoe to kiss his chin, Sadie giggled. "*You're* his father. Do whatever you think is best."

Gently laying a hand on each of her cheeks, he kissed the tip of her nose. "*You're* the counselor. What do you advise?"

She looked at some invisible spot over his shoulder, considering his question. Sadie was smiling softly when she met his eyes again. "I think you're going to need to break it to him in stages." Grinning mischievously, she added, "He's a smart kid, and I think he's figured out that we. . .uh. . .like each other." Then, "But I don't think he's aware just how serious things have become."

Chuckling, Solon said, "Serious! Wearing a smirk like that, how can you even *say* the word?"

She ignored his playful mocking. "I think he likes me, so. . ."

"Likes you!" Solon laughed at that. "Why, the kid *adores* you."

Waving the compliment away, she continued. "I think he likes me, so I don't think he'll have a problem with our. . . relationship." Staring deep into his eyes, she wrapped her arms around his neck. "First you have to tell him how we feel about one another. Give him a couple weeks to get used to the idea before you spring the rest of the news on him. He's been through a lot in the last few years, and we don't want to overwhelm him. And until Jesse knows," she warned, wagging a maternal finger under his nose, "no one can know."

Resting his chin on the top of her head, Solon nodded. "I suppose you're right." He took half a step back, lifted her chin on a bent forefinger. "But it's gonna be awfully hard, keeping it a secret."

"Yes," she whispered, "I'm so proud, I want to shout it to the world!"

"I guess we can use this in-between time to work out the details."

"Details?"

Shrugging, he said, "You know. . .like when and where, formal or informal, your place or mine. . .Are you certain we have to wait a whole year?"

She nodded. "Jesse deserves to have that time with you all to himself." She sighed. "Oh, Solon, I'm so excited I could pop!"

"Please. Don't. I saw what you ate yesterday. . .and then today. . ." He rolled his eyes. "We'd be here 'til midnight, cleaning up. . ."

Resting her cheek against his chest, she wrapped her arms around his middle. "All right. I get the picture." She stood still, then looked up at him. When she met his eyes, hers were glistening with tears. "I'm happy, Solon. Really happy."

"Me, too." He quirked an eyebrow, then said, "Will you keep your maiden name? For business reasons, I mean?"

Frowning and smiling at the same time, Sadie clucked her tongue in exasperation. "Of course not! I'll be *proud* to tell folks I'm Mrs. Solon Turner!"

"Mrs. Solon Turner. Sadie Turner." He grinned. "I like the sound of. . ."

The trill of the telephone interrupted them, and Sadie reluctantly stepped away from the warm comfort of his embrace to silence it. "Hello," she sang into the mouthpiece.

"Is Mr. Turner there?" a female voice asked.

"Why, yes. He is. Just a moment please."

Sadie held the receiver out to Solon. "It's for you. I wonder how they got my number?"

"Stop looking so puzzled," he said, grinning as he took the phone. "*I* got your number the moment I met you." He put the receiver to his ear. "This is Solon Turner. . ."

Sadie watched his wide smile dim, as the joyful light in his eyes vanished. Instinctively, she stood beside him, laying a reassuring hand upon his forearm.

"Yes," he said, nodding. "I understand. Do anything you feel necessary. I'll be there in ten minutes."

"What's happened?" Sadie said to his back as he hung up the phone.

When he faced her, there were tears in his eyes. "Jesse," he managed to say. "He's at Shock Trauma." Gathering her close, he stammered, "He's. . .he's been. . .he's been shot. . ."

Sadie gasped. She closed her eyes tight and prayed, *Give me strength, God. This man doesn't need my tears right now. He needs me to be strong. Make me strong enough that he can lean on me. . .And oh, loving Jesus, take care of Jesse.* She took a deep breath, and then she held Solon as he cried into the crook of her neck. *Best to let him get some of this out of his system now*, she reasoned, *because there's no telling what he'll have to stand up under once we get down there. . .*

"Solon," she said softly, and when he raised his head, she added, "will you let me drive you?"

He straightened, rubbed his eyes with the heels of his hands. "Yeah," he croaked out, "you drive." Taking the keys to the Ford from his pocket, he dropped them into her palm, closed her fingers around them, and squeezed gently. "Could be a long night," he warned, his voice cracking with emotion. "You sure you want to be stranded down there without a car? You could follow me in your car so you could. . ." His voice trailed away as though he couldn't remember what he had been about to say.

Laying her hand atop his, she lifted her chin a bit. "I'm not leaving you there alone, Solon," she insisted. "Now, why don't you get our jackets while I write a note so Mama won't worry?"

By the time he returned from the closet in the front hall, she'd scribbled on the board stuck to the refrigerator: Mama—Solon and I are with Jesse at Shock Trauma. I'll call as soon as I know something. She drew a heart, then signed her name.

❧

Jesse had been in surgery for nearly three hours, and Solon hadn't sat down once in all that time. His nervous pacing would wear him out, even if the emotional strain of the night didn't, Sadie believed. She knew him well enough to know he'd never rest for himself. But if he believed it was for *her*. . .Maybe it was time now for her to stop being so strong.

"Solon," she said, blocking his path. "I'm starting to get scared." It was true, after all, despite the reasons she'd admitted it. She looked down the long, empty hall at the double doors leading to the operating suite. "It's been so long, and. . ."

Just as she'd expected, Solon draped an arm over her shoulders. "Come on," he said, guiding her to the row of chairs along the wall, "let's get you off your feet." Once she'd taken a seat, he added, "Can I get you anything? Coffee? A soda?"

Sadie wrapped her arms around him. "Nothing, Solon. Just you."

They sat that way, locked in one another's arms, until a deep, resonant voice interrupted them. "Mr. Turner?"

Solon and Sadie stood, still clinging to one another.

The man thrust out his right hand, and Solon took it. "I'm Dr. Rolnick. Sorry we didn't have a chance to discuss our options earlier, but you were in transit when we took your son into surgery." He released Solon's hand. "Your son is in recovery now." The doctor removed his sweat-stained, tight-fitting green cap and ran a hand through his thinning dark hair, then gestured toward the chairs. "Let's have a seat," he instructed, dragging one to face the rest.

Like obedient children, Sadie and Solon took their seats and waited for the doctor's prognosis.

"I believe in getting the bad news out of the way first," he began, "but let me state, right up front, that the bullet missed the heart and the aorta. It did a considerable amount of tissue damage, and he lost a lot of blood, but he's young and strong and healthy, and there's no reason to anticipate complications."

He quickly explained that the bullet had entered high, and angled up, hitting and shattering the lower edge of the clavicle. The upper pectorals had been injured, along with the rhomboid and trapezius muscles of the upper back upon exit. The deltoids of the upper arm and lower shoulder had also been affected slightly. "But considering he was hit with a .357 at close-range, your son was lucky. Very lucky," Rolnick emphasized.

Solon nodded. "Will there be any permanent damage?"

Rolnick shook his head. "Too soon to tell. In a week or so, when the healing process has begun, we'll start him on physical therapy. It's going to be a long slow road, I have to tell you that right now. But off the record, I'd say he has an excellent chance of recovery."

"When can we see him?" Solon asked.

"Soon as he's out of recovery, I'll have a nurse come get you. He won't look good," he warned, "not after what he's been through, and he'll probably still be unconscious. But I promise the worst is over now."

Solon let out a deep breath of relief. "Thanks, doc."

The doctor rose, as did Solon and Sadie. He shot an understanding smile over his shoulder. "I usually make rounds at about ten in the morning. I'll talk to you more then."

He hadn't been gone two minutes when a policeman stepped into the space Rolnick had just vacated. "Mr. Turner, I'm Officer Whitworth." As Rolnick had done, the cop shook Solon's hand. "Sorry to have to put your through this right now, but I'm going to need some information from you."

Solon shook his head, ran a hand over his hair. "Sure. Sure. Anything."

The cop fired a volley of questions at him, and when he left, Solon slumped into the nearest chair. He sat there, scowling and silent for several moments, then bolted upright. "When I find out who did this to Jesse. . ." On his feet now, he resumed pacing like a caged tiger. This time, anger—not fear and worry—propelled him. "Whoever did this is a dead man," he snarled, flexing his fists.

ôô

When at last the nurse came to tell Solon that Jesse was out of recovery, Solon totally ignored hospital policy and pulled Sadie into the cubicle with him. "You're going to be his mother in a few months," he said with a gritty determination. "You have as much right to be here as I do."

"There's just no sense arguing with you when you get like this, Solon." She smiled lovingly when she said it, to show him she was fully prepared to deal with his obstinence. . .forever.

They stood beside the narrow bed where Jesse lay and watched his labored breathing. His golden-brown complexion had turned ashen gray. Surgical tape secured the oxygen tubes to his nostrils. Bottles of glucose and antibiotic hung from a wheeled aluminum stand, their clear tubes carrying nourishment and medication to his wounded body.

"He looks so small, so innocent and *young*, lying there with his eyes closed like that," Solon said softly. "Reminds me of when he was just a little boy, and he'd fall asleep after I'd read him a bedtime story." Shaking his head, he added, "So young. . .and helpless. . ." He looked at her, cocked an eyebrow, and tucked in one corner of his mouth. "I hate hospitals," he admitted. "They make me feel scared and . . .vulnerable."

She linked her fingers with his. "Me, too. But maybe it doesn't hurt to us acknowledge every now and then that we aren't as much in control as we like to think we are." Her gaze darted to the ceiling, as though she could see the Holy Spirit hovering over them. "We're in God's hands—now when life seems bad and scary, just as much as when we think we got life right where we want it in the palm of our hand." She leaned against him and whispered, "So long as we're in the Lord's big old hands, we're safe, Solon. And so is Jesse. No matter what."

He gave her hand an affectionate squeeze. "I know you're right. But I—" His voice broke and he forced himself to swallow the bitter words that hovered on his tongue. God hadn't kept his son safe. No, God had let him down. Again.

A nurse bustled into the room, the sleeves of her starched white lab coat swishing as she crossed the floor. "There's another policeman waiting to see you," she said, directing his attention toward the door.

Solon looked where she'd pointed. "Tell him he'll just have to wait."

"Now, Mr. Turner, let's not be difficult," she admonished, a finger in the air, "I've already let you stay way past the allotted time." She headed back for the nurses' station. Grabbing the curved door handle, she paused. "You don't want to lose 'favorite' status, now do you?" Shooting a half smile in his direction, she pulled open the door, and left them alone with Jesse again.

"We may as well talk to him," Sadie suggested. "You look like you could use a cup of coffee, anyway."

Smiling warmly, he released her hand. "I suppose you're right." Solon leaned over the bed and pressed a light kiss to his son's forehead. "I love you, son," he whispered, smoothing the boy's matted hair. Then, straightening, he took Sadie's hand again and nodded toward the cop. "Let's go find out what he wants."

The moment the doors to the ICU hissed shut, the cop said, "Officer Jordan." He wrapped Solon's hand in his own. "Can I have a word with you?" He glanced at Sadie. "Alone?"

Solon opened his mouth to protest, but her raised hand

silenced him. "I'm going to get us some coffee. Would you care for a cup, officer?"

He shook his head. "No. But thanks all the same, ma'am." The young man stood, fidgeting with his watchband, his notebook, his ballpoint pen as he waited for Sadie to leave. The moment she was out of earshot, he said, "According to what your son told the paramedics on the ride in, the shooter was one Rasheed Potts. He's one bad dude," said the cop, shaking his blond head. "Got a rap sheet longer 'n' my leg."

Solon wanted to find out all he could about the lowlife who'd tried to murder his son. But he couldn't let the cop see his own anger, an anger that was close to murderous in its intensity. Choosing and enunciating every word carefully, precisely, he quizzed the officer. "What's the name of the gang he belongs to?"

"He's no ordinary member. Potts *founded* the Bloods."

"Funny," Solon said, innocently wrinkling his brow. "I've never heard of them. Which neighborhood are they from?"

"The Bloods have all but taken over Leakin Park."

Leakin Park, eh? Solon narrowed his eyes and ground his molars together.

❧

He'd been walking the dark, rain-slicked streets for nearly two hours before he spotted a ragtag bunch of boys gathered in the doorway of an abandoned building near the park. "Any of you ever hear of a brother goes by name of Rasheed Potts?"

"What's it worth to you?" the biggest one asked.

Solon scowled, shrugged. He read the malicious intent in their eyes and knew if he named a dollar amount—even a small one—they'd kill him right where he stood to get it. From the looks of on their angry, defiant faces, they might kill him anyway, just for sport.

He'd come here to seek vengeance, but not if it meant making an orphan of Jesse. Solon bit back his fury. He would not tell this surly youth what sizzled on his tongue: if he *didn't* help him find Rasheed, it might be worth *his* life.

"Left my wallet at home," he said instead, turning first his jacket pockets and then his jeans pockets inside out to prove it.

"What you want with Rasheed?"

The pent-up rage threatened to boil over. He gritted his teeth to summon control, then said in a gritty voice, "We have business to discuss."

The kid who'd been doing all the talking stepped forward. "What kind of business?"

There were five of them, one of him. Solon dismissed the odds. "Unless you're Rasheed," he snarled, "it's none of *your* business."

The kid snickered, looked at his friends. "Ha! Check this fool out." As suddenly as it had appeared, the boy's smile vanished. "I'm Rasheed," he said, taking a long drag from his joint. "So what you want with me, man?"

He'd imagined it a thousand times since taking that call from Shock Trauma. Like lightning flashes, the images were emblazoned on his brain: This ruthless, sneering boy. The powerful gun. Jesse, left to die in a pool of his own blood. . . The thought of his son, suffering and afraid. . .

Any control Solon had mustered died, right where he stood. Rage roiled inside him, turning anger into hatred. Growling like a maniac, he lunged forward, reaching for Rasheed's throat.

"Hey, man, you crazy or somethin'?" the leader demanded, ducking Solon's grasp. "Why you comin' at me like a wild man?"

Glowering, the muscles in Solon's jaw tensed. "Because," he said, emphasizing each and every word, "I'm Jesse Turner's father, that's why."

Rasheed, standing a safe distance away now, raised his arms, let them slap against his sides. "Well," he said, rolling his eyes, "least now I know why you actin' all crazy-like."

Solon wanted to slap the smug smirk from his face. Wanted to beat the contemptuous gleam out of his eyes. And so he pounced a second time, bellowing like a wild beast as he charged forward.

No amount of marijuana could have numbed Rasheed's brain to the point where he didn't recognize blood lust when it stared him in the eye. He felt the breeze of Solon's fist as it sailed past his cheek. Dodging it, Rasheed darted from the building's entrance and ran, full speed ahead, into the black Baltimore night.

Solon took off after him, a crazed luster gleaming from his eyes. *You can run, but you can't hide for long*, he thought as the soles of his sneakers slap-slapped against the wet pavement.

He saw Rasheed duck into the building on the corner, and deliberately he slowed his pace. He didn't want the Bloods' leader to hear his approach, didn't want Rasheed to hear him enter the building. Stepping carefully into the gloom, he kept his back to the wall, listening, watching, waiting. . .

Inside, the evidence of new construction lay all around him, from the scent of fresh-cut lumber to the powdery piles of sawdust peppering the wood beneath his feet. The light of the halogen lamp outside slanted through the tall, narrow window and across the floor, creating eery, misshapen shadows of sawhorses, ladders, and an assortment of power tools on the makeshift workbench against the wall.

Standing stock-still, he strained his ears toward the soft sound that slip-slided across the gritty plywood-planked floor. Outside, in the distance, he heard the hiss of tires passing over the damp street. The occasional blare of a car horn. The far-off whine of a siren. Inside, Solon could almost hear the thundering of his own heart as the adrenaline-pumped blood pulsed maddeningly through his veins.

When at last he identified the source of the noise that had captured his attention, Solon grinned, his face hard. Rasheed, he believed, was hiding very near. The grin slanted to a leer as he thought, *He's right around the corner. . .*

Solon crouched on the floor and leaned against a sheet of

drywall. He was prepared to wait there all night, if necessary, to make this boy pay for what he'd done to Jesse. He had a strong suspicion that wouldn't be necessary, for a boy like Rasheed likely possessed less patience than a pampered toddler.

In minutes, it seemed, he heard the sounds of padded footfalls moving closer, closer. . .He got to his knees, then to his feet, ready for battle. The instant Rasheed's hulking form came into view, Solon spotted the shadow of the gun. . .likely the same one that had blown a hole the size of a man's fist in his boy's chest.

Knowing that very soon now he'd have to defend himself, his gaze frantically scanned the workbench in search of a weapon. Forcing himself to move slowly, so as not to give away his position, he reached out and wrapped his fingers around a familiar tool—a nail gun. He gave its cord a gentle tug to determine whether or not it was plugged in.

It was.

He lifted the tool and let it rest against his hip. It barely touched a brass brad on the seam of his jeans. The quiet metallic *click* echoed through the room.

Immediately, Rasheed swiveled, gun arm stiff as he pointed the weapon toward the sound. With the instinct and cunning of a mountain cat, he immediately zeroed in on his prey, and aimed the gun directly at Solon's chest. Through the shadows, their gazes locked, forming an invisible, taut thread of violent intent.

Understanding that his only chance of survival against the power of a .357 was the element of surprise, Solon raised his own "weapon". . . and fired it.

The whispered *ffftt* of the nail he'd sent sailing through the air broke the silence. Rasheed's bellow filled the room. In the ensuing beat of silence, Solon saw that his shot had miraculously pinned the cuff of the boy's blue satin jacket to the wall.

In no time, Solon knew, a boy this big and burly could wrest his sleeve free—but, being big and *dumb*, Rasheed hadn't yet realized it. . .

Seizing this temporary reprieve, Solon lunged forward, used his left hand to grab a handful of shirt, his right to shove the startled boy against the crossbeams. "Don't move," he rasped, pressing the nail gun into Rasheed's temple. "Don't even breathe. And drop the gun."

A half dozen times, Rasheed tried to bolt from Solon's powerful grasp. Half a dozen times, the older man slammed him back against the wall like a rag doll. "Drop it, I said," Solon whispered between his teeth. "Unless you'd like your head nailed to this wall."

The gun clattered to the floor, but Rasheed continued to twist against Solon's grip. "Let me loose, man, or. . ."

Chuckling malevolently, Solon ignored him. "You disappoint me, Rasheed," he said, tightening his grip on the shirt. "With all your drug money, I'd think you could afford to buy yourself a stick of antiperspirant." He sniffed the air. "You're sweating like a pig, and you smell like one, too."

"You bluffin'," Rasheed repeated, unable, it seemed, to focus on anything but the tool that was pressed against his temple. "Spoiled, rich man like you ain't got what it takes to. . ."

Grimacing, Solon moved his hand a fraction and fired a second shot, sneering when Rasheed lurched with fright as a ten-penny nail embedded itself in the wood beside his ear. "If I were you," Solon grated, "I'd shut my mouth and I'd *keep* it shut." Spittle flew from his lips as he raged on, and his nose was nearly touching Rasheed's when he said, "You tried to kill my son; you don't know *what* I'm capable of doing, you miserable little. . ."

Rasheed's terrified eyes darted back and forth in their sockets, then widened and calmed a bit before his gaze settled on something just over Solon's right shoulder. The corners of his mouth pulled up in a trembly grin.

Solon knew what the expression meant. But he ignored the terror that gripped him. "Feelin' brave, now that all your little soldiers are here?" He pointed the nail gun at Rasheed's forehead. Through clenched teeth, he said, "Tell them this thing is loaded, Rasheed. Tell them if they so much as blink, you're a dead man." He aimed the tool past the boy's left ear and let a nail loose, just to show the rest of the gang that he meant business.

A pitiful little bleat passed Rasheed's lips in response to the third shot fired. His eyes widened still further, and his voice cracked when he said, "Don't none of you do nothin' stupid. This fool's crazy. . ."

"You boys read the Bible?" Solon asked, never taking his eyes from Rasheed's.

"I read it some, when I was a kid," Mohammed said.

"Did you ever read the verse that says 'an eye for an eye'?"

"I guess. . ."

Solon aimed the gun at Rasheed's right eye, and smiled sardonically. "Well, you tried to kill my boy. And I plan to do the same to you. Only I'm aiming to succeed. . ." He let a second tick by before adding, "You better say your prayers, boy," he growled.

Rasheed licked his lips. "Get off me, man. Let me go. You is one *crazy* fool. They gonna lock you up in Shepherd Pratt and throw away the key. . ."

"What's wrong, Rasheed? Don't you remember any prayers?" Laughing calmly, he added, "Maybe your *brothers* will help you." Then, to the Bloods, he said, "You gonna pray for old Rasheed, here? You gonna ask the good Lord to bless his sorry soul and throw open the gates of heaven?"

A moment of mingled snickers and chuckles gave Solon the answer to his question. He touched the nail gun to Rasheed's cheek. Shaking his head, he singsonged, "Tooooo baaaad. Looks like your brothers don't care much *where* you end up when I get through with you."

"B-But. . .but th-that's only 'cause you told 'em if they moved, y-you'd. . ."

He fired a nail into the two-by-four just to the left of Rasheed's ear. "They've got guns, just like yours," he rasped. "If they'd wanted to stop me, I'd be dead by now, and you know it."

A moment of silence passed. "Ain't that right, boys?"

The Bloods did not respond.

"I gave you a chance to say a prayer. . .Now it's time to say *good-bye*, Rasheed. . ."

The boy's perspiration-soaked shirt began to quake in Solon's grasp. Grimacing, he glared at the terrified boy. "How's it feel to be scared, huh? How do you like somebody bigger, somebody better armed, somebody more powerful, threatening *you*?"

"I. . .I d-don't like it," Rasheed whimpered, closing his eyes.

"Look at me when I'm talkin' to you, boy!" he commanded, shooting another nail. This time it landed between Rasheed's feet.

Rasheed opened his eyes. "I don't w-wanna l-look at you, man," he stammered. "You is a *crazy man*!" The husky boy trembled, so hard he would have fallen except for Solon's hold on him. "P-please," he begged, struggling to free himself from Solon's death grip, "don't shoot m-me with that thing." Sobbing uncontrollably now, Rasheed pleaded, "Don't kill me."

His words penetrated the fog of fury that had blotted all reason from Solon's mind. Just as he'd been able to picture Rasheed's bullet piercing Jesse's chest, he saw himself now. . .

As a spotlight illuminates a stage, the street lamp lit the space where he and Rasheed stood. In the glowing oval, Solon saw the boy, back still pressed tight against the crossbeams, arms outstretched like a strange and sick rendition of Christ on the cross. *You're about to nail Me to the cross all over again, Solon,* a voice whispered in his mind.

Solon was suddenly nauseated. Christ and this lowlife had

nothing in common; Christ had been innocent and this boy certainly was not. And yet. . .in trying to mete out his form of vigilante justice, Solon realized he was in danger of becoming like the boy he so reviled. I died for this boy just as much as I did for you, Solon, whispered the small voice.

"I'm not going to risk my happiness, my family's happiness, by killing you," Solon said, his voice thick. His knuckles ached when he let loose of Rasheed's shirt. Flexing his fists, he said, "You're just not worth it, not to me." He heard the echo of that quiet voice he'd heard, and he added, "You're in God's hands, Rasheed. And I'd say you better be begging for His mercy."

He stepped back and let the nail gun slide from his fingers. When it landed with a *clang*, he turned and began to walk away. The Bloods stepped further into the room, giving Solon plenty of berth to pass, and stood nearer their shaky leader.

Rasheed, reading the looks of shock and disgust on the faces of his brothers, ripped his sleeve free of the nail that had pinned him to the wall. "I don't need nobody's mercy." He bent to retrieve the .357 from where it had landed. Gripping it with both hands, he extended his shuddering arms and took aim at Solon.

As his right forefinger nestled into the sleek curve of the silvery trigger, the thumb of his left hand went up, arched, rested on the tip of the hammer, and flattened as he pulled the hammer back, back. . .He tensed, listening for the familiar click that would tell him it was time to pull the trigger.

But he never heard it. Never had a chance to cock the hammer all the way. Never had a chance to pull the trigger. For Mohammed had unsheathed his garish-toothed hunting knife. . .and jammed the blade between Rasheed's ribs.

The Bloods' leader stood frozen for a moment, then looked down at his oozing wound. In the next instant, he met Rasheed's eyes. "Why, man?" he asked.

Mohammed did not answer, but Rasheed would never

know this, for he was dead before Mohammed jerked his razor-sharp weapon free.

Solon, unaware of what had just gone on in the silvery silence behind him, stepped out into the drizzly darkness. He turned right and walked to his Ford.

The Bloods stared for a moment at their fallen leader, then shuffled woodenly out the door, and without a word, headed for the four winds.

ten

Soon after Coral's death, her husband and son had paid weekly visits to her grave, but the visits had been so painful for Solon that he had soon begun to find excuses for not going. He couldn't remember the last time they'd gone to the cemetery, so Solon was surprised when Jesse's first words to him this bright, early May Saturday were, "Dad, I'd like to go and see Mom's. . ."

They had gotten in the car and had been riding along in companionable silence for several minutes before the boy spoke again. "Can I ask you a question?"

"Shoot," his father said and winced at the ugly memories the word awakened.

"You've been real quiet ever since I came home from the hospital. . .is something wrong?"

Solon thought instantly of the scene in that dark row house. Although months had passed since then, and Jesse's recovery had been nearly miraculous, Solon's shame, guilt, and humiliation still reverberated in his mind. . .and in his heart. He hadn't spoken of what he had done in that house the night Jesse was shot, hadn't told anyone what he had nearly done, not even Sadie. But like the ringing repercussion of a tuning fork, that night continued to vibrate in Solon's soul. He was never free of it; it interfered with everything else in his life.

"You want to talk about it?" his son asked.

Despite the mood this trip—and his memories—had set, Solon couldn't help smiling a bit at the crack in Jesse's voice: His boy was becoming a man.

"So. . .do you want to tell me what's been bothering you?"

Solon repeated the boy's question in his mind. His son was growing up—that much was evidenced by the fact that, after seeing his father's distress, he had extended a helping hand—but was Jesse mature enough to hear about the despicable things his father had done?

Casting a brief glance in his son's direction, Solon reached across the console and tweaked the boy's hair. "You're a good kid, Jess," he said. "Have I told you that lately?"

Jesse grinned. "Only about ten thousand times. If I had known my getting good grades would make you this easy to live with, I would have done it years ago! Course there wasn't much else to do in that hospital room 'cept study."

Laughing quietly at the good-natured razzing, Solon looked through the windshield at the familiar parklike setting of Ferndale Gardens. Boxwood hedges and rose vines, clumps of birch, and groves of weeping willows grew strong and stately from the sea of lush lawns. The occasional ancient oak provided shelter for songbirds, while lilac and forsythia bushes invited rabbits and chipmunks to make their homes in the safety offered by their thickly twining branches.

Like the stiff and immovable guards at Buckingham Palace, headstones of gray and pink granite, of ivory and black marble, kept a vigilant watch over the softly mounded earth that was the final resting place for those who had gone on to meet their Maker. Row after row of these silent sentries stood amid verdigris angels, wrought-iron benches, and the occasional American flag. Each marker wore as its badge of honor a written tribute to the individual over whom it watched. Solon's wife's read: Coral Clarice Turner, beloved wife and mother. She will live on in our hearts.

"Well," Solon said, parking the Ford near Coral's grave, "we're here."

"I wonder," Jesse began, staring somberly at his mother's tombstone, "why people spend so much money on death. I mean, they taught us in Sunday school that once you die, your spirit leaves you, and all that's left is the shell that was your body." Moving his good arm left to right, Jesse indicated the hundreds of markers that dotted the horizon. "Just *look* at all of 'em," he said. "Some of 'em look like the statues in the art museum." Meeting Solon's eyes, he concluded, "They must have cost. . ."

". . .a small fortune," Solon finished for him. "Your mama's for one. . ."

Together, they surveyed Coral's marker, four feet high, three feet wide, and a foot thick, and carved of pure-white Italian marble. To the left of one gently rounded corner stood a guardian angel, her delicate hands wrapped around the stone the way a mother's hands wrap around her newborn's bassinet. Solon looked into the angel's face, remembering exactly why he'd commissioned this tombstone. . .she wore the same expression he'd seen so many times on Coral's sweet face as she held their baby boy to her breast, a look that combined the wonderment of motherhood with the determination to take the responsibilities of parenthood seriously.

Watching Coral wither and die had stood him apart from God; he had found no serenity at her passing, no sense of peace in eternity's promise, and so he'd bought the most expensive coffin, the biggest basket of flowers, the best headstone, thinking that if all of it didn't buy eternal comfort for Coral, perhaps it would buy it for *him*. No, he had not known peace at her passing. But he knew it now.

Or he had until the ugly moment when he had almost taken God's vengeance into his own hands.

Jesse seemed so surprised to learn that his father had invested "a small fortune" in his mother's burial site that Solon was inspired to say, "She was a good wife. A wonderful mother, and what a big-hearted woman!" He spoke as much to himself as to Jesse. "Seemed she was always thinking of ways to help others, always doing something kind and caring. Not once did she keep score of the good deeds she'd done. Never did she expect *quid pro quo*."

"Huh?"

"It's a fancy way of saying 'you scratch my back and I'll scratch yours,'" he explained, chuckling. "Your mother was the kind of woman who liked to stand in the shadows, watching and listening, to find out what a person needed. And then, she'd find a way to meet that need." He met his son's eyes to add, "Most of the time, folks never knew what she'd done."

His gaze returned to the stone as he said, "She always gave her level best, so I gave *her* the best."

Jesse was looking at the stone, too, when he asked, "You loved her a lot, didn't you?"

"More than life itself," his father said, his voice raspy with memories.

Solon's wistful smile was mirrored on his son's face. "Sounds like you still love her."

"Always will, I expect."

Jesse turned toward him. "Then is it fair to marry Sadie? I mean, I've seen the way she looks at you, Dad. . . like she's staring into the face of an angel or something. She's in love with you, big time."

Solon smiled. He'd seen the expression Jesse described. . . many times. And many times, he'd wondered what he'd ever done to deserve it. Though he didn't expect to ever get the answer to that question, Solon had decided to accept the gift of Sadie's unconditional, all-encompassing love. And, though he didn't expect to ever be worthy of her devotion and dedication—especially not after what he'd almost done in a moment of rage—still, he'd spend the rest of his life trying to make her happy.

"Does Sadie know how you feel about Mom?"

"Yes, she does."

Jesse's voice was incredulous when he said, "And she still wants to marry you? How come she's not jealous?"

"You already answered that one, Jess." He tweaked the boy's hair again. "She loves me."

"But. . ."

". . .but your mama is a sweet memory that I'll treasure 'til I die. . ."

". . .and Sadie is a livin', breathin' woman who loves us both. . .*now*," Jesse said, nodding as comprehension emerged.

"Exactly."

"Are you guys gonna have kids together?"

Solon blinked with surprise at the question. "Well, Jess, the truth is, we haven't discussed it yet. How would you feel if we did?"

"Are you kiddin'?" Jess snickered. "A little brother or sister to bully and tease. Who *wouldn't* love it?"

Chuckling, Solon pulled his son close. "I love *you*, Jess. Have I told you that lately?"

"Only about ten thousand times. . ."

Solon and Jesse made their way to a white bench near Coral's grave. Side by side, father and son considered their separate thoughts.

Five, perhaps ten minutes ticked by before Jesse spoke. "So, Dad. . .when are you gonna tell me about it?"

He knew without asking what the boy wanted to know. But Solon asked anyway, "Tell you about what?"

After expelling an exasperated sigh, Jesse rolled his eyes. "About whatever has been eating at you. Didn't you tell me when I was in the hospital that we'd never keep things from each other anymore?"

What Solon had *meant* when he'd given that particular little speech was that Jesse should feel free to come to him, any time, about any subject, and they'd discuss it openly and fair-mindedly, like friends. But to admit that now would sound an awful lot like do as I say, not as I do.

"Look, Dad," Jesse began. "Whatever it is, it can't be that bad. You'll feel better if you talk about it. I promise."

Solon gave him a crooked grin. Hadn't he said exactly that to Jesse, not two days ago, when he saw his boy moping and worrying about his feud with Carleen? Solon sighed. He didn't want to share that ugly night with his son—and yet something told him it was the right thing to do. He took a deep breath and plunged in.

Once he got started, it was as though he didn't know where to stop. He spelled it all out, from the moment he'd taken the call from Shock Trauma to the morning after when he had heard on the news that Rasheed Potts had been found stabbed to death. *Might be good for the boy*, Solon thought, *to see that adults can make mistakes. . .and have to come to terms with them too*.

When finally the tale was told, Solon heaved a deep relieved sigh and leaned back on the bench, exhausted. "Well, I hope you're happy now," he said, slipping an arm over Jesse's good shoulder. "Now you know—your old man has weaknesses and. . ."

"All I know," the boy said emphatically, "is that my dad is human, and I love him." He gave a shy smile. "God loves you, too, Dad. So why don't you just forget about it now? You didn't kill Rasheed, and that's what counts."

Their eyes met for an instant, and in that instant, father and son knew instinctively that nothing but death would ever separate them again. Solon heaved a sigh. He felt as though a huge load had been lifted from his shoulders. *I can forgive even the greatest sins, remember?* a familiar, small voice whispered in his heart. *That's why I came. That's why I died.*

❧

Hannah and Floyd had decided to exchange vows on Mother's Day in a quiet church ceremony, with only family and close friends present. Since they'd both been married before, neither felt the need for an elaborate reception. And that's how it happened that Sadie's minuscule backyard became a banquet hall.

She'd gone all out for the event, just as she had for their big Thanksgiving celebration. Only this time, Sadie wouldn't give the weatherman the upper hand: she saved her prettiest, most fragile decorations for inside, and decorated her yard with pastel balloons, so that rain or shine, her handiwork would not be ruined.

Her sister looked beautiful in her classic-cut, off-white

linen suit. She wore matching pumps and wrist-length gloves, but the outfit wouldn't have been complete without the perky little hat perched just off-center on her well-coiffed head. She carried a bouquet of three red roses to represent the love of her children and her husband.

As the wedding guests browsed and chatted, Sadie flitted through the small crowd, delivering refreshments and clearing discarded cups and plates from the wrought-iron tables scattered across her yard. As she moved about, she caught snatches of conversation: Pastor Higgins would retire on the first of the year; Mrs. Jones, the church organist, had become a great-grandmother. . .for the tenth time! Samantha Davis and Sebrina Thomson bickered over who'd win "Best of Show" in this summer's Flower Mart. And Juanita Reynolds had just been appointed director of the Calvary choir.

But the main topic of discussion during the wedding reception had been Hannah's announcement that, despite her husband's generous salary, she had no plans to stay home full time after returning from her month-long European honeymoon. Her own children would both be enrolled at Bradley High in the fall, she'd explained, and certainly didn't need her hovering over them before and after school. As for her *students*. . ."I just *love* those little ones!" Hannah insisted, "and I can't imagine life without 'em!" A natural-born teacher, Hannah belonged in a classroom; a natural-born mother, she needed to surround herself with small children.

The only subject that came close to competing with Hannah's decision to continue working had been news that Kinder Kare would close its doors on the last day of school in June. Several of the women who would be out of work when that sad day came were present at the reception.

Their disappointment ended when the bride clapped her white-gloved hands and commanded the attention of her company. She announced that Floyd had helped her open a business called "Barnes Academy."

Hannah and Solon had put their heads together and concocted

the job-saving scheme. He called in a few favors, and pulled a few strings, and the result—after Floyd's hefty investment— was a suite center on the first floor of the World Trade Center. Employees of every company conducting business in the city would have access to the day care center. . .of which Hannah would be director!

Sadie beamed at the newlyweds. . .and her own soon-to-be husband. *The Lord works in mysterious ways*, she told herself as the guests cheered Hannah's good news. Winking as she smiled at her petite sister, she added, *good things come in small packages*.

And when Solon caught her eye, she thought, *Love is kind . . .and beareth all things, believeth all things, hopeth all things, endureth all things.* Even in a world fraught with the worries of feminists, it would be the easiest thing Sadie had ever done to surrender her life to this wonderful man.

❧

With Hannah's wedding over, Sadie turned her attention to the next major event on her agenda: the Builder's Ball. She'd been looking forward to the black-tie dinner for nearly a month now, searching in every mall between Baltimore and Washington, between Baltimore and Lancaster, Pennsylvania for the right dress for such a special occasion. She was beginning to understand how Hannah must have felt, all those months ago when Floyd invited her to the Peabody and she could find nothing to wear. Sadie had plenty of business suits and more than enough dresses. But the clothes in her closet, while completely appropriate for work and church, could not begin to meet the sophistication requirements of the prestigious and elegant Builders' Ball.

Just when she was about to give up and hire a seamstress, Sadie found the perfect gown. She hadn't even been looking for clothing the day she passed the tiny shop in Ellicott City. She'd driven west on Route 40, taking a right at Ridge, and another right onto the nation's first legitimate highway, Frederick Road. Once she reached the historic city's shopping district, the street name changed to Main Street. She was looking for a birthday gift for her secretary today, and for the moment she had forgotten about the Builders' Ball.

As she browsed through the quaint streets, something in a store window commanded a second look. . .then a closer look. . .The dress—pale blue chiffon, trimmed with a narrow band of the same blue satin—hung from the mannikin like liquid sky. The filmy material fluttered in the faint breeze, reminding Sadie of the wings of cherubim and seraphim.

As she went inside the shop, the owner, having seen Sadie admiring the dress, clomped down the aisle on knee-high brown suede boots. Her long, gauzy skirt swung around her ankles as she planted herself beside her customer. "Oh, do try it on," the woman said. "I have a feeling it'll be perfect for you!"

When Sadie stepped out of the fitting room wearing the gown, the woman raised such a ruckus, Sadie believed the lawyers having lunch down at the Judge's Bench likely heard her. "You look like a fairy princess," the woman gushed. "Like Disney's Pocohantas. Or Jasmine." Folding her hands contemplatively beneath her chin, she smiled and closed her eyes.

When she got the dress home, Sadie removed the cover of the shiny pink cardboard box and laid the matching tissue aside. For a moment, she only looked at the gown. When finally she lifted it from its bed of crumpled paper, she held it to her chest and closed her eyes.

She wanted nothing more than to please Solon, to be beautiful in his eyes, to make his life a haven from the stresses and strains of the world. And she wanted to make him proud, too, on his very special night.

Since he'd learned he was in line to receive the Builders' Best award, Solon's company had been written up in all the newspapers, and he'd been interviewed on every local TV station. He'd tried to shrug off the fame, explaining it away as the fickle and short-lived attentions of the media. But Sadie had seen the pride in his dark eyes when the envelope from the Builders' Association had arrived. "We are pleased to inform you that Turner Construction is one of four companies nominated to receive the Builders' Best Award," the letter began. "You'll be proud to know that you were chosen from more than two hundred candidates. . ."

Though he hadn't said a word as he refolded the letter and slid it back into the envelope, Solon had been walking with a new spring in his step ever since. She knew that just being nominated was quite an honor; still, Sadie wanted Solon to *win* that award!

On the night of the big gala, hours before Solon was to pick her up, Sadie primped and preened in the wide mirror above her vanity. She wanted everything to be perfect, from the top of her head to the toes of her blue-satin high-heeled shoes.

"Sadie," Faith cried as her daughter descended the staircase, "you have never looked lovelier. That man's eyes are gonna pop clean out of his head when he gets a look at you." Smiling with pride, she shook her head. "Mmm-mmm-mmm," she said, "clean out of his head, I tell you!"

Sadie was about to tell her mother not to make such a big fuss when the doorbell rang. She'd known him over a year now, so why did she feel like a schoolgirl in the throes of a mad crush? Laying a hand over her hammering heart, Sadie took a calming breath as Faith opened the door.

The sight of him, standing there on her tiny stoop in his tuxedo and carrying a red-ribboned white box, sent her heartbeat into overdrive. *What did you ever do in your miserable little life to deserve a fine man like* that, *girl?* she asked herself. The question went unanswered; the answer didn't matter. What mattered was that she'd deserve him *from now on*. She was going to love him and his son with all her heart and strength.

"You're beautiful," he said, his voice soft and raspy. "I'll be the envy of every man at the Builders' Ball."

How could any woman look into eyes that beamed with adoration as Solon's did now, and not want to give her life to

her man? Sadie wondered. In her mind. . .and in her heart. . .
the things she planned to do for Solon once they were married would not lock her in a submissive role. Rather, because
the gestures would be born of love and performed with joy,
they'd underscore her position of equality in the marriage.

"And you look beautiful, yourself. Mama," she said, winking at Faith, "where's that cane the doctor gave you when
you sprained your ankle last year?"

Faith's brow furrowed with confusion. "Why, it's in the
front hall closet, there. But what do you want with that nasty
old thing?"

Eyes on her man once more, Sadie stepped into the warmth
of his embrace. "He looks so fine, I'm gonna have to beat the
ladies off with a stick!" she explained, smiling up into his
face.

Gently, Solon kissed her cheek. "Don't want to muss your
makeup," he said. "But just you wait 'til I bring you home
again. . ." To Faith he said, "Don't turn on the porch light
when you turn in. . ."

☙

The fact that they'd managed to find a parking place so near
her front door seemed just one more blessing. They sat in the
front seat of his Ford, the light misting down from the street
lamps outlining their clasped hands with a silvery glow. . .
and glinting from the polished brass plaque in Solon's hands.

"I've been working toward this for more than a decade,"
he admitted.

"Then it's a well-deserved trophy, I'd say."

He met her eyes. "You really think I sounded okay up
there? When I gave my acceptance speech, I mean. . ."

Sadie smiled and patted his hand. "You sounded like you'd
done it a hundred times. You looked so calm and collected. In
fact," she inserted, "the lady beside me asked where you took
voice lessons, where you learned your public speaking skills."

"Go on," he said, grinning. "You're just saying that to
make me feel better."

Sadie shook her head. "I am *not!* I was so proud, watching you up there at the microphone."

Solon took a deep breath. "Feels good, having earned this. But. . ."

"What do you mean, 'but. . .'?" she exclaimed. "How can there be a 'but' on a night like this?"

Shrugging, he confessed, "Now that I've got it, all eyes are on me." He met her eyes. "How do I top *this?*"

"Men!" she said, smiling playfully. "It hasn't been an hour since they put that plaque in your hands, and already you're worried about losing it. You can't be Number One out there," she said, pointing to the world on the other side of the windshield, "not *every* year. Just keep doing everything you did to win it *this* year, and you'll always be Number One with me."

Leaning over the console, he drew her into a hug. "I love you, Sadie. You're a gift from God."

"Well, loosen your grip on the package," she said, giggling, "'cause you're crushing the wrapper."

Solon loosed his hold a bit. "I was proud of you, too, tonight." He sat back, held her face in his hands. "When we walked into that banquet hall, every head turned in your direction." Grinning, he added, "You were the belle of the ball!"

"Did you ever consider that maybe they were looking at *you?*"

He shook his head. "Not a chance. Line up all those men and make 'em face the wall, nobody could have told us apart. But you, all decked out in that gorgeous get-up. . . you'd stand out in a crowd of ten thousand females!"

Sadie shivered. "It's chilly for a June night."

"Let's get you inside, then." He started to open the door, but stopped. "Wait. I want to show you something first. . ."

Flipping on the overhead light, he reached into the back seat and retrieved a three-foot-long roll of papers. "Take a look at that."

"Blueprints?"

Solon nodded. "Go on. Tell me what you think."

Sadie removed the rubber band, slid it onto her wrist, and unrolled the plans. The first page laid out the first and second floors, the second sheet described the basement and potential third floor. The third. . .and last. . .a blue-lined sketch of a Victorian-style house, complete with a three-sided wrap-around covered porch. On the left side of the house, a turret; on the right, a two-car garage.

It was the house she'd always yearned for. But she'd never shared the dream with Solon; how could he have known? she wondered, meeting his eyes.

"Your mama showed me a picture in a *Better Homes and Gardens* magazine," he said, answering her unasked question. "I thought it might be awkward for Faith, living with us after we're married. And since she seems so happy here, I hoped maybe we could sell my house, and use the profits to pay off the mortgage on this place." He nodded at the drawings. "If you like it, we can get started right away; it'll be finished by Thanksgiving. . .nearly a month before our wedding. . ."

"*If* I like it," she gasped, her eyes on the blueprint once more. "Solon, I *love* it!" She flipped back to the first page. "How big is the kitchen?" she wanted to know, running her finger along the shaded blue lines. "Is it big enough for a table and chairs? What about windows? Are there plenty of windows?"

Chuckling, he pulled her against his chest again, crumpling the pages in her lap. "Solon," she protested weakly, "you're wrinkling my. . ."

"I'm sorry," he said, relaxing his hug. "Didn't mean to wrinkle your pretty dress."

Grinning with excitement, she furrowed her brow. "Dress . . .who cares about any old dress? You're wrinkling my dream house!"

epilogue

eight years later

"Solon," Sadie said, wiping her perspiring brow with the heel of her hand, "what time is it?" She sat back on her heels in the garden's soft soil.

He set aside his measuring tape and square and looked at his watch. "A quarter after two. . .exactly fifteen minutes since the last time you asked," he said, chuckling. "Why the sudden interest in the clock. . .got a hot date or something?"

Feigning a haughty grin, Sadie only shook her head.

Left brow high on his forehead, he narrowed his eyes. "Uh-oh. I'd recognize that look anywhere." Tucking in one corner of his mouth, he pointed his grease pencil at her. "'Fess up, Sadie. What's goin' on?"

The innocent expression she wore now was no less pretended than the supercilious one had been earlier. Elbows tight against her narrow waist, Sadie held out her hands. "'Fess up? Going on?" Tilting her head flirtatiously, she blinked and smiled. "Why, Solon, I haven't the faintest idea what you're talking about."

Shaking his head, he grinned. "You're probably not old enough to remember the Ink Spots," he said.

Wrinkling her brow, she squinted and tapped a finger against her chin. "Weren't they a singing group back in the forties?"

Hands flat on his workbench, he nodded. "Some of their tunes went to the top of the Hit Parade charts. . ."

The phony expressions she'd sent him moments ago were replaced now by a look of genuine confusion. "I don't get it . . .what do the Ink Spots have to do with. . . ?"

"Do you still contend there's nothing going on around here

161

that I should know about?"

"Yes," she said carefully, "but I still don't see what that has to do..."

Solon closed his eyes and stood tall. "'It's a sin to tell a lie,'" he crooned off-key, using his pencil as a microphone.

Sticking her fingers in her ears, Sadie winced. "Solon, please...the neighbors will think we've adopted an orphaned beagle pup if you keep up that howling!"

Chuckling, he focused on the blueprint he'd tacked to the workbench earlier. "All right...I know when to surrender." Without looking up, he added, "But consider yourself warned: I hate surprises..."

Wearing a smug smile of satisfaction, Sadie, too, got back to work in her garden. With a little cooperation from nature, her vegetable garden would be a raging success this year. Already, her leaf lettuce and spring onions were up, and the first green shoots of snow peas and radishes had begun to sprout.

She loved the garden Solon had created for her at the back of their two-acre yard. To protect the tender shoots from the rabbits, chipmunks, and deer living in the wooded glen behind their lot, he'd secured chicken wire to the white picket fence that surrounded the twenty- by forty-foot patch. Last year, her tomatoes had been the envy of the neighborhood. Why should this year be any different?

On her hands and knees, Sadie raked through the dark, silty earth with a short-handled, three-pronged fork, pulling weeds and picking stones. *Consider yourself warned,* he'd said, *I hate surprises...*

As if she didn't know better! Why, she'd studied his every move, his every *mood,* almost from the day they'd met all those years ago. She could tell the moment he walked through the door what kind of day he'd had—good or bad— just by reading his face. And no matter how hard he tried to disguise the everyday stresses and strains of his job when he called home from the office, she could tell if things weren't going well because her ears were attuned to even the most subtle changes in the tone and timbre of his voice.

"'I hate surprises,' indeed," she muttered under her breath as she patted the soil tight around the roots of her plantings.

"What's that, sweetie?" he asked.

Sadie grinned at the absentminded sound in his voice. He was so lost in his project at that moment, that even if she *had* spilled the beans. . .and told him every minute detail of what she *did* have planned, Solon wouldn't have heard it.

The thought of his latest project made her heart throb with love for her big, generous husband. Soon after they moved into the house, he'd discovered she had nowhere to keep her collection of seashells. And so he'd made her a curio, complete with etched glass doors and lighted shelves. As it turned out, he was quite a craftsman; since then he had designed and built the furniture in the family room as well. Now he was hard at work on a desk for Jesse's new apartment.

Don't you worry your li'l punkin head, Solon, she said to herself. Smirking at her own ingenuity, she added, *But this is* one *surprise you're going to love, sweet man!*

❧

"Dad, can I watch TV now?"

Solon shook his head. "Have you finished your homework?"

"No. . .but it won't take me long, and I thought a little TV break would help me concentrate on it later. . ." The little girl smiled winningly up at her father.

Smiling, Sadie continued to chop the Vidalia onion, knowing even before she heard his voice what her husband would say. "That's a wonderful and imaginative answer, Yolanda." He quirked a brow and grinned. "Now, do your homework!"

The girl planted her elbow on the kitchen table, rested her cheek in her palm. "It's no fair," she huffed, pouting. "Homework is boring."

Smiling, Sadie met Solon's eyes. Oh, how she loved that man! He'd always been such a good, decent man, and every day since they'd exchanged vows, he'd given her more and more reason to call him a wonderful husband. As she watched him now, in the chair beside his daughter, patiently but firmly helping her sort out the problems in the textbook, she was reminded again that Solon had been born to be a father.

Sighing deeply, the little girl said, "I don't know why we even need to study this stuff. . ."

"Because it'll make a better person of you, that's why," Solon told her. "Even if you only make use of half of what's in that book," he said, pointing at the hard-bound math volume, "doing the work will help develop discipline. Without self-discipline. . ."

". . .we're no better than the animals," his daughter said with him. Gripping her pencil between the first and second fingers of her left hand, she allowed the eraser to tap, tap, tap on the pages of her math book.

"You may as well just get busy," Solon told her, "because the longer you sit there wasting time, the longer—"

He was interrupted by the triple blast of a horn and then a car door slam.

"Who can that be this close to supper time?" Sadie asked, drying her hands on a red-gingham tea towel.

Solon parted the sheer curtains covering the back door's glass panel and peeked onto the porch. His hand was on the brass knob when the door flew open. "Well, if that don't beat all," he said to their unexpected visitor.

"Who is it, Dad?"

"It's me, that's who!"

The little girl leaped up from the table so fast, her chair nearly toppled over. "Jesse!" she shouted. "What are you doing here?"

Dropping his duffle bag near the door, he scooped his little sister up into his arms and planted a loud wet kiss on Yolanda's cheek. "Since when do I need a reason to come see my little sister?"

Giggling, Yolanda wrapped her arms around Jesse's neck.

"How long can you stay this time?"

Grinning, Jesse winked at Sadie. "Through the weekend, anyway."

Yolanda frowned slightly as she fingered the collar of Jesse's plaid shirt. "Won't you get in trouble at the hospital?"

"Naw, the nurses at Chicago General were glad to get rid of me for a couple of days," he said, gently depositing Yolanda back onto her chair. "Now, what's all this?" he asked, peering over the little girl's shoulder.

As if she were a marionette whose puppeteer had just dropped her strings, Yolanda sagged onto the table. "Homework," she complained. Then, in an even grumpier tone, "*Math* homework. . ."

"Ah-ha." As his father had done so many times with him, Jesse tweaked Yolanda's hair. "I thought you liked math."

"I *hate* it. It's hard and it's boring and. . ."

Squatting beside the seven-year-old's chair, Jesse said, "I thought you wanted to be a doctor, like I'm going to be. . ."

The girl's eyes widened. "I *do* want to be like you, Jess. I just don't want to do math."

"How you gonna be a doctor if you won't do math?" he asked, narrowing his eyes.

The girl considered this for a moment. Brightening, she said, "I'll get one of my nurses to do it!"

Laughing, Jesse hugged his sister. "Do your homework, li'l sister. You don't have to like it," he winked, "but you have to do it."

Pouting and bobbing her head from side to side, Yolanda rolled her eyes. "All right," she agreed, retrieving her pencil. Grinning, she added, "What's seven times eight. . . ?"

Laughing, Jesse gave her a playful shove. "*You* figure it out!"

Sadie took Jesse's hand. "It's good to have you home, son." She put a maternal hand alongside his face. "You look thinner. And tired. I'll bet you're up all hours and eating fast food." She held out her arms.

"It's good to *be* home," he said, stepping into the warmth of her embrace. Over her shoulder, he met Solon's eyes. "How's it goin', Dad?"

"Good. Real good," he said. Joining the hug, he added, "Lots better, now that you're home."

"Where's Micah?" Jesse asked once the circle of welcome had broken.

"Upstairs, taking a nap," Sadie answered. She took a deep breath. "Four days out of five, I can't get him to sit still, let alone lie down and sleep, so I'm enjoying these afternoon respites as much as I can for as long as they last!"

"I'm surprised he's still napping at all at three years old," Jesse said. "Way I hear it, I never did take naps."

"Until you turned thirteen," Solon put in. "Then we couldn't seem to *keep* you from sleeping!"

Chuckling, the younger man walked over to the stove and lifted the lid on the big aluminum kettle. "Mmmm-mmm-mmm," he sighed, eyes closed as he inhaled the steam. Sending another wink Sadie's way, he said, "My favorite. . . spaghetti."

Solon narrowed his eyes. "Say. . .we haven't had spaghetti since. . ."

". . .since the last time Jesse came home," Yolanda announced.

Solon crossed both arms over his chest. "Seems to me there's more cookin' round here than that sauce, there. . ."

"Well, if nobody minds," Jesse said, picking up his duffle bag and heading for the hall, "I'm going up to see if Micah is awake. If he's not, I might just join him!"

"Supper's not 'til seven," Sadie called after him. "You have plenty of time for a nap."

Solon took Sadie in his arms. "You've been acting strangely all day. Now," he said, his lips grazing her cheek, "why don't you tell me all about it. I promise, you'll feel better if you do. . ."

She pressed a quick kiss to his lips. "Solon Turner, I told

you earlier there's nothing to tell, and there *still* isn't."
Suppressing a mischievous grin as she stepped away from
him, Sadie picked up the serving spoon she'd rested on a
saucer near the stove and began stirring the contents of her
pot. "Needs something," she said, smacking her lips and
frowning as she tasted it. "What do you think?"

He allowed her to feed him a bite of the thick red sauce.
"Mama mia, that's even better than ham hocks and chit-
tlens!"

"Ugh!" Sadie winced. "Solon, you know I hate ham
hocks."

Solon narrowed one eye. "You sure you're black, girl?"

Ignoring his teasing grin, Sadie clucked her tongue. "It's
startling how much alike you and Jesse are beginning to
sound. He's already a good inch taller than you; once he fin-
ishes his internship and gets some decent food and rest, I
think he'll pass you on the scales, too." She pointed at the
spoon. "Well, what do you think?"

"I think *somebody* has something up her sleeve, that's
what I think. . ."

&

Solon clasped his hands under his neck and stared up at the
night-black ceiling. "Supper was terrific. And that birthday
cake. . .It's a wonder all those candles didn't set off the
smoke alarms." Laughing, he patted his stomach. "You keep
feeding me like that, I'm gonna get fat and lazy."

"You? Never!"

For a while, neither of them spoke, content even with
these sweet, quiet moments of married life.

"Funny," he said after a while. "I don't feel forty-six."

"Well, you're not of course. Not 'til tomorrow. How else
could I have surprised you? But you better not feel forty-six
then either."

He could barely make out her profile in the darkness of
their room. "What do you mean?"

"If you looked forty-six," she said, digging her fingertip

into his ribs, "I might have to trade you in on a younger model!"

Wrapping both arms around her, he kissed her soundly. "Sadie," he said, "I never thought I'd be saying this. . .but I'm happier than I've ever been in my life. Please don't take this the wrong way—but I used to think that you were just sort of Coral's substitute. I thought she sent you to me."

Sadie giggled good-naturedly. "I realize the woman was a saint, Solon, but even she hasn't got that kind of power."

"I know that now." Absently, his fingertips caressed her shoulder as he spoke. "You're a gift from God."

"He's not a very imaginative gift giver, then."

"Why, Sadie Turner!" he gasped. "I can't believe anything so sacrilegious could pass your sweet li—"

She lay a finger against his mouth to silence him. "The good Lord knows exactly what's in my heart." She smiled. "You're a gift from God, too, you know."

His expression, his tone, even his touch gentled as he looked into her eyes through the darkness. "I've never been happier," he said again. "And I don't think life could get any better."

Sadie rolled onto her back and tidied the covers. "Well, things might not get better, but I have a feeling they're going to get more. . .um. . .interesting."

"Interesting? What do you mean?"

"Well, I took a test today and. . ."

Solon sat up and threw back the covers, then turned on the lamp on the bedside table. Hands on her shoulders, he gave her a gentle shake. "We're going to have another baby!"

She shook her head. "No, Solon," Sadie whispered. "we're not going to have another baby."

Solon's shoulders sagged and the joy in his eyes dimmed. "Oh. Well. Sorry." He forced a happy grin. "Didn't mean to get all excited over nothing." Suddenly, he seemed to recall that she'd said the word *test*. Gripping her tighter, fear glinted in his eyes. "You're all right, aren't you? Why did you have a test? Why didn't you tell me? I'd have come with you."

Sadie climbed onto his lap. "Solon," she began, taking his face in her hands, "we're not going to have a baby. . ."

As the furrow between his brows deepened, her smile grew.

". . .we're going to have two."

A moment of silence passed as he stared, barely blinking, into her face. In the next moment, tears shimmered in his eyes, and a trembly smile tugged at the corners of his mouth. He buried his face in the crook of her neck. "'And behold,'" he quoted Genesis, "'there were twins in her womb. . .'"

"I never thought I'd live to hear you reciting Bible verses in bed," she said, laughing through her own happy tears.

He kissed her eyes, her cheeks, her chin. "Did you ever read Proverbs?"

"Dozens of times. It's one of my favorite books of the Bible."

"Mine, too," he acknowledged, nodding. "And you'll find the verse I'm thinking of in Proverbs, chapter thirty-one, verse ten."

Smiling, she dried her eyes.

"Go on. Get the Good Book," he said, nodding at the nightstand.

She crawled across their mattress and, lying on her stomach, slid open the drawer where she kept her much-used old Bible. Sitting Indian style then, she found the verse: "'Who can find a virtuous woman, for her price is far above rubies. . .'"

"The whole chapter describes *you*, Sadie. 'The heart of her husband doth safely trust in her. . .she will do him good all the days of her life. . .Strength and honour are her clothing . . .She opens her mouth with wisdom. . .She looketh well to the ways of her household. . .'"

She'd been reading the chapter right along with him, but she closed the Bible now and returned it to the nightstand drawer.

"'Her children arise up,'" Solon continued, "'and call her blessed; her husband also, and he praiseth her. . .'"

Sadie drew the covers up over them and gently pressed his shoulder until he lay down beside her. "'They are glad because they be quiet,'" she quoted Psalms.

Smiling lovingly into his eyes, she pressed her lips to his. "Now, will you please turn off the light, Solon. . . ?"

A Letter To Our Readers

Dear Reader:

In order that we might better contribute to your reading enjoyment, we would appreciate your taking a few minutes to respond to the following questions. When completed, please return to the following:

Rebecca Germany, Managing Editor
Heartsong Presents
P.O. Box 719
Uhrichsville, Ohio 44683

1. Did you enjoy reading *Soft Beats My Heart*?
   ❑ Very much. I would like to see more books
      by this author!
   ❑ Moderately
      I would have enjoyed it more if _____

   _____

2. Are you a member of **Heartsong Presents**? ❑Yes ❑No
   If no, where did you purchase this book?_____

   _____

3. What influenced your decision to purchase this
   book? (Check those that apply.)

   ❑ Cover   ❑ Back cover copy

   ❑ Title   ❑ Friends

   ❑ Publicity   ❑ Other_____

4. How would you rate, on a scale from 1 (poor) to 5
   (superior), the cover design?_____

5. On a scale from 1 (poor) to 10 (superior), please rate the following elements.

___Heroine   ___Plot

___Hero   ___Inspirational theme

___Setting   ___Secondary characters

6. What settings would you like to see covered in **Heartsong Presents** books?_____

_____

_____

7. What are some inspirational themes you would like to see treated in future books?_____

_____

_____

8. Would you be interested in reading other **Heartsong Presents** titles?   ❏ Yes   ❏ No

9. Please check your age range:
   ❏ Under 18   ❏ 18-24   ❏ 25-34
   ❏ 35-45   ❏ 46-55   ❏ Over 55

10. How many hours per week do you read? _____

Name _____

Occupation _____

Address _____

City_____ State_____ Zip_____

Cook "Inn" Style

with *The Christian Bed & Breakfast Cookbook*

A companion volume to the popular *Christian Bed & Breakfast Directory*, this tantalizing cookbook includes the "specialties of the house" from bed and breakfast establishments across the United States and Canada. With over 500 pages of recipes such as "Breakfast in a Cookie," "Irish Soda Bread," and "Mississippi Fried Pies" featuring serving suggestions, garnishes, and the history or origin of most recipes, it's more than a bargain at $3.97.

528 pages; paperbound; 5" x 8"

Hearts♥ng

HEARTSONG PRESENTS TITLES AVAILABLE NOW:

_HP 37 DRUMS OF SHELOMOH, *Yvonne Lehman*

_HP 38 A PLACE TO CALL HOME, *Eileen M. Berger*

_HP 41 FIELDS OF SWEET CONTENT, *Norma Jean Lutz*

_HP 49 YESTERDAY'S TOMORROWS, *Linda Herring*

_HP 50 DANCE IN THE DISTANCE, *Kjersti Hoff Baez*

_HP 53 MIDNIGHT MUSIC, *Janelle Burnham*

_HP 54 HOME TO HER HEART, *Lena Nelson Dooley*

_HP 57 LOVE'S SILKEN MELODY, *Norma Jean Lutz*

_HP 58 FREE TO LOVE, *Doris English*

_HP 61 PICTURE PERFECT, *Susan Kirby*

_HP 62 A REAL AND PRECIOUS THING, *Brenda Bancroft*

_HP 66 AUTUMN LOVE, *Ann Bell*

_HP 69 BETWEEN LOVE AND LOYALTY, *Susannah Hayden*

_HP 70 A NEW SONG, *Kathleen Yapp*

_HP 73 MIDSUMMER'S DREAM, *Rena Eastman*

_HP 81 BETTER THAN FRIENDS, *Sally Laity*

_HP 82 SOUTHERN GENTLEMEN, *Yvonne Lehman*

_HP 85 LAMP IN DARKNESS, *Connie Loraine*

_HP 86 POCKETFUL OF LOVE, *Loree Lough*

_HP 89 CONTAGIOUS LOVE, *Ann Bell*

_HP 90 CATER TO A WHIM, *Norma Jean Lutz*

_HP 93 IDITAROD DREAM, *Janelle Jamison*

_HP 94 TO BE STRONG, *Carolyn R. Scheidies*

_HP 97 A MATCH MADE IN HEAVEN, *Kathleen Yapp*

_HP 98 BEAUTY FOR ASHES, *Becky Melby and Cathy Wienke*

_HP101 DAMAGED DREAMS, *Mary Hawkins*

_HP102 IF GIVEN A CHOICE, *Tracie J. Peterson*

_HP105 CIRCLE OF LOVE, *Alma Blair*

_HP106 RAGDOLL, *Kelly R. Stevens*

_HP109 INSPIRED LOVE, *Ann Bell*

_HP110 CALLIE'S MOUNTAIN, *Veda Boyd Jones*

_HP113 BETWEEN THE MEMORY AND THE MOMENT, *Susannah Hayden*

_HP114 THE QUIET HEART, *Rae Simons*

_HP117 FARTHER ALONG THE ROAD, *Susannah Hayden*

_HP118 FLICKERING FLAMES, *Connie Loraine*

_HP121 THE WINNING HEART, *Norma Jean Lutz*

_HP122 THERE'S ALWAYS TOMORROW, *Brenda Bancroft*

_HP125 LOVE'S TENDER GIFT, *Elizabeth Murphy*

_HP126 MOUNTAIN MAN, *Yvonne Lehman*

_HP129 SEARCH FOR YESTERDAY, *Mary Hawkins*

_HP130 A MATTER OF SECURITY, *Kay Cornelius*

_HP133 A CHANGE OF HEART, *Nancy Lavo*

(If ordering from this page, please remember to include it with the order form.)

.... Presents ....

__HP134 THE ROAD HOME, *Susannah Hayden*

__HP137 DISTANT LOVE, *Ann Bell*

__HP138 ABIDING LOVE, *Elizabeth Murphy*

__HP142 FLYING HIGH, *Phyllis A. Humphrey*

__HP145 MOCKING BIRD'S SONG, *Janet Gortsema*

__HP146 DANCING IN THE DARKNESS, *Janelle Burnham*

__HP149 LLAMA LAND, *VeraLee Wiggins*

__HP150 TENDER MERCY, *Elizabeth Murphy*

__HP153 HEALING LOVE, *Ann Bell*

__HP154 CALLIE'S CHALLENGE, *Veda Boyd Jones*

__HP157 POCKETFUL OF PROMISES, *Loree Lough*

__HP158 ON WINGS OF SONG, *Brenda Knight Graham*

__HP161 MONTANA SKY, *Loree Lough*

__HP162 GOLDEN DREAMS, *Kathleen Yapp*

__HP165 CONSIDER HER WAYS, *Fran Vincent*

__HP166 A GIFT FROM ABOVE, *Dina Leonhardt Koehly*

__HP169 GARMENT OF PRAISE, *Becky Melby and Cathy Wienke*

__HP170 AGAINST THAT DAY, *Rae Simons*

__HP173 THE HASTY HEART, *Helen Spears*

__HP174 BEHIND THE SCENES, *Gloria Brandt*

__HP177 NEPALI NOON, *Susannah Hayden*

__HP178 EAGLES FOR ANNA, *Cathrine Runyon*

__HP181 RETREAT TO LOVE, *Nancy N. Rue*

__HP182 A WING AND A PRAYER, *Tracie J. Peterson*

__HP185 ABIDE WITH ME, *Una McManus*

__HP186 WINGS LIKE EAGLES, *Tracie J. Peterson*

__HP189 A KINDLED SPARK, *ColleenL. Reece*

__HP190 A MATTER OF FAITH, *Nina Coombs Pykare*

__HP193 COMPASSIONATE LOVE, *Ann Bell*

__HP194 WAIT FOR THE MORNING, *Kjersti Hoff Baez*

__HP197 EAGLE PILOT, *Jill Stengl*

__HP198 WATERCOLOR CASTLES, *Ranee McCollum*

__HP201 A WHOLE NEW WORLD, *Yvonne Lehman*

__HP202 SEARCH FOR TODAY, *Mary Hawkins*

__HP205 A QUESTION OF BALANCE, *Veda Boyd Jones*

__HP206 POLITICALLY CORRECT, *Kay Cornelius*

__HP209 SOFT BEATS MY HEART, *Aleesha Carter*

__HP210 THE FRUIT OF HER HANDS, *Jane Orcutt*

Great Inspirational Romance at a Great Price!

Heartsong Presents books are inspirational romances in contemporary and historical settings, designed to give you an enjoyable, spirit-lifting reading experience. You can choose wonderfully written titles from some of today's best authors like Veda Boyd Jones, Yvonne Lehman, Tracie J. Peterson, Nancy N. Rue, and many others.

When ordering quantities less than twelve, above titles are $2.95 each.

Hearts♥ng Presents
Love Stories Are Rated G!

That's for godly, gratifying, and of course, great! If you love a thrilling love story, but don't appreciate the sordidness of some popular paperback romances, **Heartsong Presents** is for you. In fact, **Heartsong Presents** is the *only inspirational romance book club*, the only one featuring love stories where Christian faith is the primary ingredient in a marriage relationship.

Sign up today to receive your first set of four, never before published Christian romances. Send no money now; you will receive a bill with the first shipment. You may cancel at any time without obligation, and if you aren't completely satisfied with any selection, you may return the books for an immediate refund!

Imagine. . .four new romances every four weeks—two historical, two contemporary—with men and women like you who long to meet the one God has chosen as the love of their lives. . .all for the low price of $9.97 postpaid.

To join, simply complete the coupon below and mail to the address provided. **Heartsong Presents** romances are rated G for another reason: They'll arrive *Godspeed!*